Colin's Prison

Copyright © 2013 by D.A Wearmouth

Chapter 1

Foundation and Purpose

In the beginning, Colin created Prison…

Inmates are born into Colin's Prison. They are taught the ways of Colin's Prison from a very early age. The entire physical life of an Inmate is spent in Colin's Prison until the day they die – either mentally or physically. There is no escape.

Colin will monitor every single physical action from the control room. He also has the ability to see into every intimate thought the Prisoner might conceive. There is no hiding place.

When Prisoners finally get to the gates when the living time is served, it is not the end. They will be judged on their actions and thoughts accordingly. And Colin has a plan for every single one of them.

There are two possible choices for a Prisoners' final destination, a pair of eternal dungeons which differ significantly. Depending on the conduct during the time served in Colin's Prison a decision will be made by Colin.

Colin created one of the dungeons as 'paradise', which is the Dungeon2; this place is a reward for good behaviour. The other possible destination is a horrible place and although it's boastfully claimed that Colin created everything, he will not take responsibility for Dungeon3. Neither of these two places can be seen through the bars, they have no defined location, there are no witness accounts but it's guaranteed that an Inmate will be transferred to one or the other.

There are various explanations of how and why the Prison was built in the differing Prison manuals available throughout the complex. The popular consensus is that Colin did it. For argument's sake, the most followed manual will be used throughout this book, whose Inmates are housed in C Wing. Other manuals and the behaviour of the Inmates who subscribe to these will be touched upon to demonstrate that not all Inmates are the same. Colin can be accessed through many channels.

Colin brought everything into being: Prison and every living thing. In the beginning there was nothing; within six days he shaped a world of order and beauty.

The Prison has a control room for the all-seeing and all-knowing. Six main Wings make up the Prison with some smaller blocks attached. The Prison has a power station which provides power and light. By peering through the bars into the distance it is possible to see the glow of other power stations. These are suspected to possibly support other Prisons containing more of Colin's creations. Nobody knows and Colin will not say. Are the Prisoners truly alone?

A couple of quotes are available from the creator during this period from the C Wing Prison manual. Firstly Colin said, *"Let there be light,"* when initially switching on the power station and powering up the Prison.

Secondly, he modestly decided, *"Let us make Prisoners in our own image."* What is unclear from the second quote is who Colin was addressing and whether he acted alone. Somebody had to hear him say it. But who?

The outcome was that Colin is credited with creating a male and female Inmate in his own likeness and giving them authority over all living things. As both the male and female Prisoners were created in his likeness, it is difficult to speculate exactly what Colin looks like.

Colin looked at everything he had made and was very pleased. He took the 7th day off.

When studying Colin's design, there are two unexplained, troubling items. Both will ensure the future destruction of all Inmates and the Prison itself in violent circumstances. Is Colin bothered that the Prison, along with all of its inhabitants, are due to be obliterated?

The power station will eventually go into meltdown, which in turn will engulf and consume the Prison in a huge red ball of heat. Evidence can be seen by peering through the bars into the far distance and observing the lifespan of other power stations. Nothing can stop this event from happening. What supports the Prison now is a ticking time-bomb.

The power station is not the only guarantee that the Prison will be annihilated in the distant future. A distant mobile Prison system is also heading straight towards Colin's apparent favourite creation at a rapid speed; this can also be observed through the bars.

The collision will smash the Prison and destroy any living thing. One way or the other, it's an undeniable fact that Colin's Prison will cease to exist in the future.

Is the lifespan of the power station or the deadly direction of the distant mobile Prison system sloppy design work by Colin, or part of a larger plan? Colin is said to move in mysterious ways, but this seems to be far more sinister and menacing. According to a Prison manual though, this is not just a case of sheer incompetence, Colin knows the exact hour when the Prison will perish:

Concerning that day or that hour, no one knows, not even the Inmates in Dungeon2, nor the Son, but only Colin.

Colin is playing his cards close to his chest on this issue of total destruction. But it will happen.

Colin's apparent pleasure at his creation did not last very long it would seem. He busily went about correcting some minor faults by wiping out ninety-nine per cent of the living species that have ever dwelled in the Prison through famine, disease, weather and dramatic extinction events. The forgiving founding father must have been crafting more space for Inmates.

Despite Colin's apparent appetite for vengeance in the form of smashing up parts of the infrastructure or killing groups of his creations though various means, Colin's job is generally viewed to be voyeuristic and judgmental.

Colin takes revenge on all who oppose him and furiously destroys his enemies! Colin is slow to get angry, but his power is great, and he never lets the guilty go unpunished. He displays his power in the whirlwind and the storm.

***

Life in Prison revolves around the belief and worship of Colin in many forms. The channels of worship are governed by pious and threatening dictatorships consisting of staff members who officially and unofficially represent Colin. Senior Inmates who have the backing of Colin through the consent of the Staff also form part of the leadership team. Manuals written in the recent Prison history provide the cornerstone for the whole system to be effective.

The popular version followed by C Wing includes a biography about the life of Colin's son Veldi along with a history section covering Colin's creative work. This particular Prison manual contains many important lessons, instructions and tales designed to teach and help the Inmates to live a good life and get to Dungeon2 once dead.

The rank structure put in place to ensure the manual is followed is fairly standard: At the top of the tree sit the most powerful of the staff. They can influence millions of Prisoners with their words, which are often claimed to have come directly from Colin. Some say they can even hear his voice directly from the control room. Normal Inmates are considered mentally ill if they claim the same. They live privileged lives and inhabit some of the most impressive places in their particular block. The senior staff usually wear luxury clothing made out of thick, rich woven material laced with trinkets and jewels. Most senior staff members are generally inaccessible to Inmates unless they decide to visit areas of the Prison outside of their layer, but their existence is undeniable. Staff are humble.

The lower ranking staff in Prison are dressed down a level from the top ranking officials of Colin. Their job in the Wings is to preach the word of Colin to anyone who will listen. They do this to hammer home the message in person for the good of the Inmates. Spreading this message may appear boring, but there is an important aspect of sly mental bullying with accompanied threats at play. The influence of the juniors should not be underestimated; although they do not have the power of the higher echelons of their Wing, they number many and have altered many lives irreversibility.

There is no avoidance for Inmates. They will believe in Colin. Colin will own their life for eternity. Everyone must love Colin and obey.

Go into all the world and proclaim the Prison manual to the whole creation. Whoever believes will be saved, but whoever does not believe will be condemned.

Throughout the history of the Prison, selective interpretation of the manuals has led to some startling behaviour through the twisting of the texts, and the consequences have been grim. But all is in the name of Colin.

Inmates and organizations in Prison have Colin on their side if they use his name; this apparently validates everything. If somebody kills fellow Inmates in the name of Colin, how could anyone disagree who also believes in Colin? Colin worshippers do not have to check with him first, so there's clearly no need for any clarification from the great creator. With Colin onside, even evil actions are justified. How else would anyone get away with doing them otherwise?

In the name of the most merciful and compassionate Colin.

***

Questions can generally not be asked about the authenticity of the Prison manuals, despite the fact that nobody in the texts could write and the manuals were written many years later, so no verifiable eye witness accounts exist.

Contradictions also number many, but the words in the manuals are sacred.

If issue is taken with some of the text, it is generally seen as a misunderstanding of the context. The previously believed story of the creation has now morphed into a metaphor. If serious protest does persist, a one-way ticket to the wicked Dungeon3 is guaranteed if Colin is not respected.

Colin is the saviour and he does not like questions being asked, as evidenced in the C and H Wing Prison manuals.

An Inmate once challenged Colin. The creator had allowed the Prisoners life to be systematically destroyed to prove a worthless point in the *Book of Boj*. The Inmate was completely unaware as to why his life was turning into a disaster, and at the height of his suffering he cursed the day he was born to a group of friends. What followed was a documented example of Colin flying off the handle. Colin bitterly responded to the person he had allowed to be shattered saying that there are so many things the Inmate does not know about how his Prison was formed or how the Prison works, and the Inmate should consider Colin greater than anything. Colin then shouted at the other three friends:

"I am angry with you... you have not spoken of me what is right."

That told them.

Colin doesn't storm into Prison and shout at a common Inmate today – he leaves that up to the qualified staff to do. When he requires his dirty work to be explained in a reasonable way, it's up to the staff to articulate the events as a message. Colin prefers a more hands-off approach and has delegated impressively.

Chapter 2

Formalising Prison

The Prison in ancient times bore little resemblance to the place that exists today. No Wings existed, no Prison manuals were available and no staff were around to guide the Inmates in the right direction. For tens of thousands of years Colin's favourite creations were blissfully unaware they were actually in Colin's Prison at all.

One would suppose Colin must have been sitting back thinking, *You ungrateful primate bastards*, as he watched the centuries tick over without even a nod in his direction. A Prison of beauty had been created and the ignorant Inmates were wandering around aimlessly under no law and no threat of eternal strife. The fate of these Inmates after finishing their first sentence is unknown.

How could Colin make the silly mistake of creating creatures that didn't even know of his existence? The simple explanation would be that the early Prison was a beta model that required some genocidal tinkering. All existing biped species were wiped out until only a single species was left. These would be the ones to whip into shape and be brought to order.

The question for Colin, now that he had tightened up the design, was how could he make the population realise they were Prisoners? Decimating most of the other species in Prison had not quite done the trick; leaving one dominant species with other edible ones around didn't seem appreciated.

Colin tried to keep down life expectancy to demonstrate control, still nothing. Perhaps showcasing his power by smashing up parts of the Prison in a terrifying manner would finally convince the dominant primates of his power? Not one bit. The levels of ungratefulness and stupidity must have been a large source of frustration for Colin.

How could Colin let Inmates know that he was watching them like a hawk and there would be serious consequences for stepping out of line? How could he scare them into behaving correctly and to show him the gratitude he deserved? This was becoming annoying for him.

Colin's patience finally snapped. There was only one thing for it: He decided to create a son named Veldi. The plan was to send

Veldi into one of the worst, most uneducated areas of the Prison to spread the word of Colin through teachings, performing a series of miracles and then being brutally executed. "They'll see," Colin probably chuckled. The time for subtlety was over and Colin would have one of his offspring in Prison to physically tell the Inmates directly.

Before hatching his master plan Colin decided he needed to run a tighter ship to clear the ground for Veldi and his message. Sending down a list of ten rules for the Prison would be a good start. Prisoners needed to know the difference between right and wrong, otherwise they might just carry on doing what they had been without Colin's permission.

Colin's logic seems sound. If there are no rules being enforced in Prison, how could people be accused of doing wrong and have the prospect of eternal misery in Dungeon3 hanging over them? It was time for formal rules to be introduced.

Colin summoned Kevin to collect his list. Kevin was an influential Inmate and would have the clout in Prison to spread the instructions:

And Colin said unto Kevin, "Come up to me into the control room, and be there: and I will give thee tablets of stone, and a law, and rules which I have written; that thou mayest teach them."

Kevin went and retrieved the tablets and returned to start teaching the Inmates. When he arrived back into the Prison yard, a party had started without him. When Kevin saw the dancing, he threw the tablets onto the floor in a jealous rage and smashed them into pieces before storming off. Colin groaned:

"Hew thee two tablets of stone like unto the first: and I will write upon these tables the words that were in the first tablets, which thou breakest."

This time Kevin managed to deliver the tablets without getting too upset. Prison now had some formal rules chiselled out by Colin. The list of ten was quite brief, but throughout the history of the Prison the stony demands have been persistently twisted in meaning from the original understanding. This has been carried out in order to keep them up to date with the evolving of Prison. The process is commonly known as Colinodernisation.

Below is Colin's confusing original Decalogue with some observations:

1.   You shall have no other Colins before me.

– These sound like the words of a paranoid and expectant future lover. It also suggests that Colin's Prison is not the only option available. Is Colin revealing something he was not supposed to? If there are other Colins around, does this mean there are other creators around? Does Colin have rivals?

A Wing Inmates still don't believe in any Colin, but they are subject to the opinions and actions of other Wings, hence they are Prisoners as well.

2.   You shall not make for yourself a carved image, or any likeness of anything that is in the Dungeon2, or that is in the Prison you now live, or that is in the water under the Prison. You shall not bow down to them or serve them, for I Colin am a jealous Colin, visiting the iniquity of the fathers on the children to the third and the fourth generation of those who hate me, but showing steadfast love to thousands of those who love me and keep my commandments.

– Colin's is not shy in admitting his jealously here. But rules are for breaking and flattery will get you everywhere. In the thousands of the buildings dedicated to Colin, images and carvings exist in a plentiful supply.

Technology was in its infancy when Colin first introduced the rules so some revision is required. It was impossible for Colin to pass down his opinion on cameras, smart phones and video recorders as he hadn't even given Inmates the inspiration to invent such devices yet.

An educated guess would be that some of the sickening backroom activity that takes place in Houses of Colin would not exactly be beneficial for the staff if they were caught in image or film, so the usage of digital devices should be considered a breach.

    3.   *You shall not take the name of Colin in vain; Colin will not hold him guiltless who takes his name in vain.*

– This one is fairly straightforward: If an Inmate bad mouths Colin then they will pay.

Has Colin got thin skin? One word said in frustration on the spur of the moment will render an Inmate instantly guilty. A slip of the tongue from a stubbed toe, caught finger or a touch of cramp could lead to the ultimate punishment.

4.   Remember the seventh day, to keep it for Colin. Six days you shall labour, and do all your work, but the seventh day is Colin day. On it you shall not do any work, you, or your son, or your daughter, your male servant, or your female servant, or your livestock, or the sojourner who is within your gates.

– Colin's generous side shines through with number four – a free day off. But is he really watching every move in Prison if he thinks all Inmates are well off enough to own a couple of servants and a house big enough to accommodate a lodger as well?

Although, it's not an official day off with no strings attached. It is Colin's day so he needs to be acknowledged for this generous gift.

5.   Honour your father and your mother, that your days may be long in the Prison that Colin is giving you.

– Number five takes a more subtle threatening tone, if you are not nice to your parents Colin will end your stay in Prison prematurely and a trip to Dungeon3 is waiting. Colin is clear that he is providing the days and can stop them if and when he chooses.

The Inmates must hope that their mothers and fathers are nice to them in order to make this rule easier to follow. Honouring a less than credible person is difficult at the best of times.

6.   *You shall not murder.*

– Self-explanatory and essential to keep good order amongst the Inmates. There is a slight problem with this rule in relation to Colin in Prison. Colin really should have attached a disclaimer that he is prepared to accept murder in his name. This rule would only apply for murder in Prison without an assumed Colin-attached endorsement.

7.   *You shall not commit adultery.*

– Fairly self-explanatory, although Colin is very vague about the rules around sex, which is reasonably understandable as Colin doesn't have any physical experience in matters of the carnal kind and is confined to watching it millions of times a day. On an Inmate's own head be it if they want to test the water and stray from this rule.

8.   *You shall not steal.*

– There can be no misunderstanding about the original intention of number eight. The staff and senior Inmates have had to get around this rule in a convenient way so as not to offend Colin. They never 'steal', they just 'claim' things that should belong to them. Land, possessions and life are all fair game in the name of Colin. This rule is generally only for petty crimes in Prison carried out by Inmates.

9.   *You shall not bear false witness against your Inmate next door.*

– This rule can't be argued with, Colin is on the money. But if not 'against' the Inmate next door, can a Prisoner bear false witness for his neighbour to hide devious acts and crimes? This would seem acceptable as long as it was not against another neighbour.

10.   *You shall not covet your immediate Inmate's house; you shall not covet your immediate Inmate's wife, or his male servant, or his female servant, or his ox, or his donkey, or anything that is your immediate Inmate's.*

– Colin confirms in the final rule that he knows the thoughts of Inmates and will judge them accordingly. He can see what they covet. As they are thrown in with the female servant, is Colin also referring to bestiality here and not simple ownership when mentioning the ox and donkey? Who knows? But this rule seems to be aimed at people with very wealthy neighbours.

The only assumption that can be made from this early section of the Prison manual is that the Inmates' behaviour was incredibly shocking before Colin stepped in. A lot of the rules seem quite basic, so what was going on?

It is easy to imagine why Colin would intervene if the Prisoners went around saying nasty things about their creator and their parents. If stealing, having sex behind their partner's back, robbing and murdering were also commonplace, then something had to be done.

If Inmates went around lying about their neighbours whilst fantasising about their wives, servants and animals, then this would have been an unsavoury situation that required addressing.

One wonders if Colin considered sending the Prisoners the same way as ninety-nine per cent of the other living creations that had existed in Prison before being unceremoniously extinguished. They must have been really, really bad.

Now that the code of conduct had been established in the name of Colin, punishment could be handed out.

Chapter 3

Colin's Two Dungeons

With the introduction of Colin-approved rules came the introduction of Colin-created consequences. Obey the rules and Inmates are fine, as far as they know. Break the rules through action or thought and the Inmates will be in serious trouble. Very serious trouble.

It is time to look at the two destinations available for performance-related transfers once the sentence in Colin's Prison is complete – Dungeon2 and Dungeon3.

There are some tips in the Prison manual about how to get to Dungeon2 which supplement Colin's rules:

Admit – that you are a sinner and in need of a Saviour

Is it almost impossible to follow Colin's rules? Even if a Prisoner tried their hardest, will there always be a way of interpreting the Decalogue to confirm an individual's guilt? Inmates are told they have to admit they are sinners and in need of a saviour. Only Colin is good.

A way of admitting personal sins in C Wing is to tell them to a strange nosey virgin through a shadowy grate.

Abandon – self-effort and realise that you cannot be saved by your works or your own efforts.

No matter what a Prisoner does, no matter what he tries, he can't do this on his own this text confirms. So what is the point of trying? Colin surely wouldn't be encouraging bad behaviour on purpose would he? No, Inmates must live under the constant spectre of being in the wrong – a lifetime as a frightened sinner.

The first two tips have done a lot to boost the power of Colin's staff.

Accept freely Veldi's payment for your sins, required of Colin.

Finally, a get-out clause. Colin's son will pay for Prisoner sins, so the prospects are now rosier, especially as there is no acceptance criteria for the sin committed. Veldi will take the lot however immoral – Colin requires it. This leaves the door open for unaccountability of the most odious kind.

Dungeon2 is seen in slightly different ways by numerous Wings in Colin's Prison, but it is agreed that it is the destination of choice and superior to the current Prison or Dungeon3.

An example comes from I Wing who greedily believe that seventy-two virgins will be waiting for them upon arrival and they will have an eternal erection in order to take full advantage.

A few questions spring to mind immediately about this hankering belief. Does it also mean that seventy-two mother-in-laws will also be included in the bargain? Does the Inmate keep the women once they are not virgins or are they available on tap for eternity? One can imagine it being a nightmare to manage, never mind to afford, such a thing. Would sleep even be possible with an eternal erection?

The more conventional view is that the Dungeon2 is not a sex-mad haven, but more of a peaceful and benign incarceration.

Dungeon2 is the ultimate end and fulfilment of the deepest Inmate longings, the state of supreme, definitive happiness.

Colin's control room runs all places: It can see all, hear all and intervene if required. Toe the line in Colin's Prison and Inmates can be transferred to Dungeon2 and enjoy the long, long spiritual solitary confinement. Hour after hour, happily thanking Colin forever.

If a Prisoner's name is not on the list for the Dungeon2 then it's time for them to start worrying.

An Inmate may not have liked their time in Colin's Prison, thinking that Dungeon2 sounds like a dull option. Both places are a tranquil picnic, however, compared to Dungeon3 – a complex of rage and hate.

Have no faith in Colin and this destination is guaranteed. Misbehave against Colin's rules and an Inmate will be risking a negative judgment when their time comes at the Prison gates.

When leaving Colin's Prison, if the dead Prisoner didn't know Colin or bother to worship him, Colin's has had enough of him:

But the wicked, who know not Colin, and obey not the Prison manual, shall be cast into eternal torments, and punished with everlasting destruction from the presence of Colin, and from the glory of his power.

Transportation is immediate to Dungeon3. Inmates are condemned to suffer an eternity of torment and fire. Colin's fingerprints are all over this place, and his evil side is shown in its full glory. Burning in pits of flames, being taunted from above, getting stabbed multiple times and vicious torture are all on the menu. Everybody gets served. Gnashing of teeth is also mentioned regularly in the manual; the staff are well-practiced in demonstrating this punishment.

***

The message is clear about gaining access to both places. Prisoners can worship Colin and live an imperfect life, commit various despicable sins and still go to Dungeon2 if there is an admission of guilt and a request for a saviour. Veldi will take the burden of the sins and Colin will be known to the Inmate. In Colin's Prison this means paying attention to the staff and carrying out their instructions.

Inmates can live a good life but ignore Colin at their peril; if they do, then they are earmarked for immediate post-Prison justice, which will be served. Not admitting guilt for minor offences can also lead to infinite pain and torture.

The sales pitch is quite convincing. The only guaranteed way to lose is to deny Colin's existence. The gamble would be for an

Inmate not to admit they were a sinner, even if they couldn't recall a single offence. Is the gamble worth taking? Probably not.

The only way to win is for an Inmate to admit to the staff that they are sinners and to worship Colin on a regular basis.

These two Colin creations have done a lot of assist the staff in intimidation of the Inmates. It's been established by the manual that it doesn't all end for Prisoners upon physical death – frightening things can happen afterwards as well. Colin owns everyone in Prison and has two extreme options on the table. The Inmates have been warned.

Chapter 4

Colin's Son

Veldi was the son of Colin according to the most popular Prison manual, and the second part of it is dedicated to his life.

The issue facing Colin was how he could transport Veldi into Prison. The method devised meant that Veldi arrived into the Prison in quite spectacular circumstances. In a rare case of direct intervention, Colin decided to impregnate a female Inmate. He also sent a ghost into the Prison to let her know what was happening and who the child was. This seems quite considerate, as it would allow the germination to be explained in a reasonable way; Prisoners were bound to be curious and questions would be asked.

Modern non-believers may sneer at this suggestion, but an explanation is that Colin is said to be everywhere, so why not in the ovary as well, performing his work? Colin had already given impressive gifts to the Inmates so this would only be a simple stocking-filler. To make all Inmates aware of the arrival of Veldi,

Colin pumped up the power in a distant station to send a signal; this was seen and understood.

Now the birth of Veldi was as follows: when His mother had been betrothed to Joe, before they came together she was found to be with child. And Joe her husband, being a righteous Prisoner and not wanting to disgrace her, planned to send her away secretly.

The text from the Prison manual above is confusing. Why did Joe assume that the female Inmate would be disgraced? Surely the son of Colin would not be cause for any embarrassment, rather the opposite would be true? Planning to send her away secretly might indicate that he wasn't fully convinced by the story? Joe eventually decided not to send the female away and Veldi was born into a family unit.

Very little is known of Veldi's early years, but it appears that Colin had either previously been enjoying a spot of sadism and his imagination had to be kept in line, or that he was going off-script in quite a callous way. Colin passed down a required modification to a ninety-nine- year-old Prisoner in the form of an instruction that the nonagenarian should slice off his own foreskin, along with his thirteen-year-old son's and all of the other men of his household. A strange request indeed. This old Inmate must have been an impressive man, fathering a child around the age of eighty-six. Perhaps a wiser choice would surely have been to instruct one of the younger men of the house if some holding down was required? The deed was carried out and this must have satisfied Colin.

The creator demanded that all baby boys would from now on be circumcised at the age of eight days old. His son was not spared:

And at the end of eight days, when he was circumcised, he was called Veldi.

Colin's plan must have been to keep his powder dry whilst building Veldi up into a credible force. This is understandable as one can't imagine anything as silly as paying attention to infantile ramblings in relation to Colin.

And the child grew and became strong, filled with wisdom; and the favour of Colin was upon him.

Eventually, Veldi decided that he had served his apprenticeship and was old enough to go into the world and spread the word of Colin. Firstly though, to prove to himself that he would not be tempted by nasty Dungeon3-inducing activities he decided not to eat.

This involved going to the remotest part of the Prison where nobody could see him and avoiding food for forty days and nights. During this time, Veldi was tempted to break his fast but declined. Following on from this seemingly pointless act, Veldi analysed the Prison and decided he would need some help covering such a wide area: the employment of Inmates to help him spread the word – around a dozen should do the trick, but probably not a baker's dozen as that might or difficulties down the line.

When morning came, Veldi called his disciples to him and chose twelve of them, whom he designated agitproparians.

Colin was pleased; everything was in place and ready to go. Veldi had his accessories and was now in a position to truly imprison the population on a much wider scale based on Colin's glorious Word.

Talking was not enough though; there had to be some proof concerning Veldi's genealogy, otherwise the risk of not being taken seriously was at stake. What better way than performing miracles? The sheep needed rounding up, and there were a number of ways which Veldi did this, according to the Prison manual.

Veldi must have assumed that the best way to demonstrate his credibility was through curing Prisoners, as this is the most talked about miracle in the manual. So as not to become boring, Veldi mixed it up a bit: Sometimes just a few casual words would cure the sick or a simple touch; at other times he used spit and mud for dramatic effect. The approach is sensible as it would create a host of grateful patients, many impressed onlookers and an extended fan base built up through word of mouth.

A discrepancy should be noted here: As Colin created all things in Prison, then the various illnesses would have to be part of the overall package. Veldi would surely not have defied his father by reversing some of Colin's work whilst spreading the good word – this seems contradictory. Was this a trick devised by both of them? Did Colin create the disease and give Veldi the cure via oratory, phlegm and soil in order to dupe Inmates? If Colin could get into an ovary then it is only right to speculate that he could get into an eyeball or a kidney. Veldi was reversing one of Colin's gifts, but was not subjected to any punishment. Large scale connivance has never been brought into question.

Healing blindness also features strongly in the Prison manual and was one of Veldi's personal favourites. It is written that Veldi simply had to touch the eyes of the sufferers and sight would be restored. This was not always so; for really tricky cases Veldi had to use more spit and mud.

The scientific understanding of blindness is far superior in Prison today than it was in manualical times. Specialists are professionally qualified in the field and have also had success. Veldi's methods were quickly deemed obsolete as nobody could reproduce his results with the same techniques applied. However, it is impossible to find any clinical trials or evidence against Veldi's triple therapy solution, so it may be foolish to rule it out just yet.

Another explanation has emerged for Veldi's seemingly childish prescription in the blindness cases. He was not physically curing blindness, he was just opening the eyes of the Prisoner to the riches of Colin. This makes more sense.

Veldi stated that the Inmate's blindness was not because either the Inmate or his parents sinned. Veldi mixed spittle with dirt to make a mud mixture, which he placed in the Inmate's eyes. Veldi then asked the Inmate to wash his eyes in a pool. This done, the Inmate was able to see.

Lepers became another favourite of Colin's son, and Veldi cured in bulk, although the unappreciative nature of some of his patients is quite disturbing.

Veldi sent ten lepers who had sought his assistance to the Prison staff, and that they were healed as they went, but only one that came back to thank Veldi.

This ungracious attitude shown towards Veldi by lepers was not a singular occurrence. As well as being an ungrateful lot, they also had a disobedient streak in them:

He once instructed the ex-leper not to tell anyone who had healed him; but the man disobeyed, increasing Veldi's fame, and thereafter Veldi withdrew to deserted places, but was followed there.

The above quote from the Prison manual is incomprehensible when Veldi's mission is taken into account. Veldi was to spread the word of Colin, so to do this he carried out miracles to rubber stamp his credentials. This in turn would surely draw attention and help spread the message by word of mouth. Why carry out miracles in secret?

Was the instruction given with a wink to the leper? Maybe not, as Veldi withdrew to deserted places. It may have been the case that fame had finally got to Veldi, which was forcing him into a career break. Veldi's popularity was growing through the use of his miraculous actions; but with attention comes a different kind of pressure.

The price of fame in modern Prison is suffocating adulation – with a sprinkling of stalking. This may well be the first documented example of a celebrity mini-meltdown. Veldi's twelve friends must have had concerns about Veldi's health and state of mind.

***

Veldi decided to soldier on. Next, he healed a paralysed Prisoner by telling him to get up and walk. The Prisoner did.

Had this antidote for paralysis been tried before? The manual is evasive about previous attempts to heal Veldi's patients, so a basic instruction could have been all that was required.

Veldi also told the same Inmate that his sins were forgiven. Whether the former disabled Inmate had murdered, had had an affair or had carved an obscure wooden Colin alternative is not known, but this story smells suspiciously like Veldi managed to flush a fraud.

Veldi also provided an admonishment for all of the alleged paralytic's crimes. This managed to annoy the local politburo who owned the franchise in the area for such things. This in turn made Veldi very angry; he said to them:

Is it easier to say that someone's sins are forgiven, or to tell the man to get up and walk?

On the face of it, both seem quite easy to say, but the following consequences are debatable. Telling an Inmate to get up and walk was a simple physical instruction requiring only a minor effort of the vocal chords. Colin's son forgiving an Inmate's sins gave the Prisoner a free pass to Dungeon2 if he died at that moment, as long as he believed in Colin. Was this a purposely loaded question from Veldi?

This all happened in a Prison cell at the time; the man had to be lowered through the roof by his friends as crowds blocked the door, due to Veldi's increasingly bloated celebrity status. The plan was working.

***

Veldi could be a good listener too, and was taught to expand his horizons beyond male lepers and blind Inmates:

An unnamed Gentile woman taught Veldi that the ministry of Colin is not limited to particular groups and persons, but belongs to all who have faith.

How did she 'teach' Veldi?

Veldi's first attempt at curing a female Inmate could have gone slightly better. This is the point where Veldi shows a touch of anatomic naivety. The understanding of the Inmate body was very basic back in manualical times.

He let a woman touch his cloak and she was instantly healed from bleeding. The knowledge of Inmate anatomy is far superior today and the likelihood was that the woman was just having her period.

After Veldi 'cured' the woman he said, *"Daughter, your faith has healed you, go in peace."* The unfortunate repercussion was that the woman would have a life of childlessness. Veldi can be forgiven for this mistake as his intentions were good. Some you win, some you lose.

Veldi's next female Inmate attempt was more successful. He healed the mother-in-law of one of his more famous employees at the time of recruiting him. How this favour convinced the Prisoner to work for Veldi is mysteriously unknown, although it was said to increase Veldi's fame so somebody benefited.

The C Wing Prison manual could not be best described as politically correct when viewed with a modern eye towards women Inmates. Compare it though to the behaviour exhibited towards the female Prisoners by Inmates from certain sections of I Wing today, and it looks like a free-spirited party.

Many in I Wing demand that the female of the species are lower ranked, and use Colin as justification for their strange misogynistic actions. Some female Inmates have Prison numbers stamped across their faces in the form of a veil. They are instructed to walk behind the male Inmate partners as second class Prisoners, and can suffer revolting punishments for less than obvious infringements. Getting stoned to death for being raped is not unheard of.

Veldi deserves some credit for not demanding this, although Colin does have something to answer for.

Copulation in Colin's Prison is permitted as long as certain rules are followed. Inmates can't have sex with themselves or members of the same sex. Fornication out of wedlock is also against the rules. Under the right circumstances, thankfully Colin has allowed the generations to continue. The manual states that Prison officials do not partake. How naïve:

We do not have a Prison official who is unable to sympathize with our weaknesses, but who in every respect has been tempted as we are, yet without sin.

This is probably a good time to take a slight break from the miracles and touch upon Veldi's sexuality. The common belief is that Veldi was asexual. From the above quote from the Prison manual it would seem that sex is a sin, so why would Veldi be even slightly interested? Modern rumours have sprung up that Veldi had a girlfriend, the main evidence being a mistaken identity from a picture that was painted hundreds of years after his life. This is abject nonsense. If any speculation was to be made at all it must surely be from the folloWing 'passage' in the Prison manual, it contains the folloWing:

A young man was folloWing Veldi, wearing nothing but a linen sheet over his naked body

What 'folloWing' means can only be speculated on; what is said is that when a mob caught this young man his sheet had 'fallen off'. Make of this what you will, but it sounds like it shares the same table as 'the dog ate my homework'. This is all quite dangerous ground for Inmates to even consider in their thoughts, so back to the miracles.

***

Veldi found a man with a withered hand inside one of the new houses of Colin who he managed to cure, having first challenged the Inmates and staff present whether it was right to do on Colin's designated day off.

Was Veldi rebelling against the control room by openly working during the day which Colin had designated for Colin worship? This angered the Prison officials present so much that they started to contemplate killing Veldi for the first time. Colin didn't react.

Veldi continued on with his mission, coming across an Inmate who was deaf and mute. A fairly straightforward job for the increasingly popular son of Colin, the standard prescription of spit was used:

He first touched the man's ears, and touched his tongue after spitting, and then said a magic word! And the man was healed.

Veldi was now becoming so powerful that all those who touched his cloak were healed. He walked through Prison corridors curing the many ill Inmates. Veldi was turning into an ancient super-antibiotic, and nothing could stand in his way. He could even cure at distance by sending people away who would find out later that their ailment had vanished.

All of this must have been starting to get to Veldi's head, as the miracles became more extreme to the point of insulting the reasoning mind. Perhaps the attention was fading after the initial impact? Inmates were losing interest as it had all been seen before. It was time for a change of pace.

The step-up in miraculous action came by the way of performing exorcisms of demons.

Veldi pointed to his ability to cast out evil spirits as a sign of his lineage, and he empowered his apparatchiks to do the same in his own name, not Colin's. This was impressive delegation – empowering his team showed a certain flare for man management. The question was, how could the twelve cronies carry out a miracle if they weren't the son of Colin and didn't have the special powers?

In one case Veldi exorcised an evil spirit who actually answered him back in a 'I know where you live' sort of way. The spirit was being cast out at the time, so it was a futile gesture on a par with threatening to kill your hangman as the trapdoor's Wings open:

"What do you want with us, Veldi of Prison? Have you come to destroy us? I know who you are – the One of Colin!"

A more spectacular example is available in the manual where Veldi started to employ new ways to impress. Would this help build the kind of credibility that ensured the word of Colin would be followed en masse?

Inmates had tried to chain up a demon but he had escaped, and lived in tombs, and roamed the complex, crying and cutting himself.

Veldi asked for the Inmate in question's name, and was told by the Prisoner that his name was Legion, *"for we are many."* Was this Prisoner schizophrenic? There can be no doubt that at least he was very sick. Veldi put forward his new and improved solution; although it was effective in expelling the demon, it failed to have the desired effect on the locals.

The Inmate asked to be expelled into a group of pigs, which Veldi allowed, and thereafter the pigs fell into water and drowned. The pig keepers told the other Prisoners what had happened, and when the Prisoners saw that the Inmate was sane, they ungratefully asked Veldi to leave for they were taken with great fear.

The next exorcism Veldi performed teaches an important lesson of how to carry out emotional blackmail. This is one of the more successfully adopted teachings carried out by Prison staff since the life of Veldi, and an important tool to keep Inmates in check.

A boy possessed by a demon was brought forward to Veldi, who was foaming at the mouth, gnashing his teeth, and involuntarily falling into both water and fire (the boy and not Veldi). This demon was serious and not for shifting. Veldi's team could not expel the demon which raised doubts around Veldi himself. Veldi's motivations for the previous delegation of duties now become clear: This was the perfect set-up to show his individual power – he was the only person capable:

Veldi condemned the Prisoners as unbelieving, but when the father of the Inmate questioned if Veldi could heal the boy, Veldi said, "Everything is possible for those that believe," so the father said he believed that the Inmate could be healed, and Veldi healed him.

A simple but effective teaching that says, 'If you don't believe in me you will be going to Dungeon3 to burn forever, and besides that little treat I will not bother healing any young Inmates either. Which way would you like this to pan out?' To believe or not to believe – that is the question.

***

Veldi had a spectacular miracle up his sleeve that was saved for special occasions. It was his hidden weapon of mass seduction; he could repatriate Inmates back to the first Prison.

An Inmate got in touch with Veldi and asked him if he would heal the Inmate's daughter. Veldi packed his case and rushed to the scene. This was a standard challenge, one he could perform with aplomb. Unfortunately on his way to the site of the potential miracle with his bag of mud, the daughter had died.

It was time to roll out the big gun. Veldi appeared, and not wanting to frighten the Inmate's father too much told him the daughter was only 'sleeping', and woke her up with the words *"Get up!"* The daughter did and was successfully brought back to life in Colin's Prison.

It was never stated which Dungeon the revived Inmate had been sent to. She must never have told anybody what the experience was like or what her chosen destination was. At least, there wasn't anybody who could be bothered to pass the information on, as there are no accounts of what happened apart from Veldi's resuscitation. Perhaps this is where the vow of silence kicks in for certain people? The incurious nature of the local Inmates appears almost unbelievable.

Veldi got a taste for this outrageous miracle and decided to carry out a few more repatriations. Rather than the unappreciative reaction Veldi received from the lepers, this time he could force people to believe and they would be grateful for him making them do so.

Veldi came across a young Prisoner who was brought out for burial in the yard. He saw the grieving mother weeping at the loss of her son, and went over either to console her or he was getting irritated by her wailing as he said:

"Do not cry."

Veldi then approached the coffin. His motivation could have been guilt or compassion, as the context of his previous statement is not explained. He told the corpse inside to *"get up,"* and he did. Another repatriation to Colin's Prison was successfully completed, which proved the miracle was no fluke.

Curiously again, questions were not asked about the experience. The revived Inmate didn't seem to care about expanding on his experience, as no accounts exist of his reactions. Only indifference would lead to a lack of other records. Was being brought back to Prison a common occurrence in manualical times?

In what initially could be viewed as an abuse of power, Veldi repatriated a personal friend of his who had been dead for four days. Simply by commanding him to *get up*, the man rose and walked around in bandages for all to see.

There onlookers learned that there was an important lesson from this show directly from Colin's son. Veldi now made sure he explained the benefits of belief, the consequence of not believing were now becoming obvious, even though left unexplained. Veldi said:

He who believes in me will live, even though he dies; and whoever lives and believes in me will never die. Do you believe this?

This quote has an irritable tone; it is known that a place in another Dungeon is promised after the first sentence is served – you are assured of an eternity in one of Colin's creations. Is Veldi threatening here to snuff out an Inmate's existence if they don't believe in him?

Did this make the much-vaunted guarantee of transportation to one of the two dungeons cast iron after all? Veldi is daring Inmates to take a risk with potentially terrible consequences, depending on which way they view the options. Believe in me or I will switch you off.

Veldi appears to have known he may have been pushing it a bit too far with his latest intimidation technique. An attempted justification was made directly to the control room by Veldi to his Father:

"Colin, I thank you that you have heard me. I knew that you always hear me, but I said this for the benefit of the people standing here, that they may believe that you sent me."

Some Prisoners were coming to the conclusion that they'd had enough. The threats, shows of power and fantastic claims were starting to become insufferable. It was undermining the rank structure that was previously in place. Veldi was now skating on thin ice.

Before leaving the miracles to find out what came of Veldi in the end, it is worth mentioning some of the more flippant and strange ones that he performed during his time in Prison. The motivation behind them is difficult to ascertain. These miracles could be attributed to a vast range of reasons, from simple convenience in order to get around a problem to experimenting out of sheer boredom with his gifts, or a sudden loss of temper. The nature of the actions is far from lucid.

Veldi was attending a Prison wedding reception when the alcohol ran out. This threatened to call a halt to proceedings and all Inmates would have to go home:

Veldi was told, "They have no wine," and he replied, "O Prisoner, what have I to do with you? My hour has not yet come."

Veldi ordered the servants to fill containers with water and to draw out some and take it to the Inmate waiter. After tasting it, and not knowing where it came from, the Inmate congratulated the bridegroom on serving the best wine he had ever drunk.

It is doubtful that Colin sent Veldi to Prison to make free alcohol, so it is difficult to draw any kind of conclusion from Veldi's actions, apart from begrudgingly carrying on the party. Binge drinking is not mentioned in the manual, and the long-term effects of drinking alcohol were not understood.

Feeding five thousand Inmates with five loaves of bread and two fish is more understandable, but hardly a miracle. Inmates will confirm that the portions are generally tiny in most popular eating establishments that feed mass gatherings.

Veldi set up another extravagant feat when he sent his apparatchiks by boat to the other side of the Prison lake while he remained behind, alone, to pray to Colin. This is one of the better-known miracles of modern times, but is the motivation behind it really understood?

Night fell, the wind rose, and the boat became caught in a storm. In the midst of the storm and the darkness the disciples saw Veldi walking on the water. They were frightened, thinking they were seeing a spirit, but Veldi told them not to be afraid; they were reassured. Veldi calmed the storm and entered the boat, and they

went on to the shore.

The reasoning in C Wing behind this act is supposed to show the importance of faith and the control of Veldi over nature.

This miracle is problematic for a number of reasons. As experienced sailors, the apparatchiks should have known better than to sail at night in poor conditions, yet they exposed themselves to the danger, while Veldi purposely stayed back onshore. Was this all premeditated?

The moral of the story seems to irresponsibly say that there is no need to formulate any kind of risk assessment when carrying out potentially dangerous activities. Have faith in Veldi because he once walked on water and controlled the weather. Was this more shoWing off or an instance of boredom leading to toying with the Prison? It certainly wouldn't help any Inmate in similar trouble at any time in the future.

The most trivial miracle was The Cursing of the Fig Tree in the Prison garden:

Veldi was hungry. Seeing in the distance a fig tree in leaf, he went to find out if it had any fruit. When he reached it, he found nothing but leaves, because it was not the season for figs. Then he said to the tree, "May no one ever eat fruit from you again."

The next day the tree was found to have withered, rendering it useless for any future passer-by. This miracle was supposed to demonstrate Veldi's power over nature again.

It is difficult to buy this explanation, as this was a petty and spiteful act considering the tree was out of season, so the chance of finding any figs to eat was zero; otherwise, what was it supposed to teach? Veldi's actions were probably brought on by hunger and frustration at the lack of food available to curb his appetite. This was not power of nature, it was a lack of understanding and abuse of nature. But apparently, Veldi didn't give a fig about it.

Veldi's temper was difficult to hide, even in a book that was written in his favour. He shouted at staff members, made thinly veiled threats to the Inmates and killed trees. All in the name of Colin.

The coin in the fish's mouth miracle was straight-out convenience. Veldi and a friend decided to enter a temple that had sprung up to honour Colin; the doorman demanded a cover charge for entrance, otherwise access was to be denied.

"So that we may not cause offense, go to the lake and throw out your line. Take the first fish you catch; open its mouth and you will find a coin. Take it and give it to them for my tax and yours."

Inmates should pay tax to the houses of Colin and they will not upset anyone, Veldi implies. It was all well and good for Veldi to say that people should pay the Colin tax – he got around the issue by miraculously producing a coin from the mouth of a fish; but others do not have this option.

Was this the first official justification for the rackets that have followed in the name of Colin? We will come to some of the more piggish exponents of this shakedown later, who have pushed the philosophy of Colin tax to enormously greedy and demented heights.

The miracles stated above in manualical times were believed for hundreds of years by the superstitious Inmates – they had no other reasonable way to explain how Veldi managed to make them come about.

Only after Inmate development in science and reasoning have the stories started to be doubted. For hundreds of years, the miracles stood as a beacon of proof that Veldi was the son of Colin. Changes were needed to keep the whole thing alive.

***

As the original claims are being viewed as increasingly unlikely, in order to make the Prison manual fit with the modern world, staff are constantly trying to come up with new ways to justify Veldi's actions. The staff mitigation comes in the form of weak metaphors or bizarre interpretations of the original claims.

A good example of this would be the explanation proposed for the cursing of the fig the tree. Probably a good one to come up with an alternative for as the original description does not exactly put Veldi in a positive light.

The tree is supposed to be a metaphor for J Wing. It had a wonderful distant appearance, but on closer inspection the tree was not producing any of Colin's fruits. Therefore the symbolic explanation for the withering tree was to show the end of the exclusive covenant between Colin and J Wing. Garbage.

Staff will say that Inmates can always casually dismiss Veldi's miracles as works of fantasy, but by doing so those Prisoners will spend the next sentence in Dungeon3 having a red hot poker rammed up their backsides, if that's what they choose. The gamble again does not seem worthwhile.

Because of the ambiguous nature of the miracles and redefining work around them, could there be another explanation possible for what really happened in Prison?

An alternative could be that Veldi was simply a very sick man in need of attention, a magician with a delusional disorder who carried out one of the most successful deceptions ever witnessed. What would Inmates think if somebody turned up today creating the same illusions?

What cannot be explained or justified is now a matter of a twisted faith in the unlikely.

***

All good things have to come to an end, and Veldi's time in Colin's Prison did just that.

The arrest, trial and execution of Veldi is somewhat of a gloomy, duplicitous affair. Conspiracy theories had been gaining momentum around the Prison for a couple of years, and it was eventually decided that he was too big for his boots and had to go. Veldi was working on the turf of other more powerful cartels who didn't appreciate his claims or popularity.

The Prison authorities needed a sneaky way to capture Veldi, and luckily one of Veldi's Fisherman's dozen decided to sell him down the river. The supper snitch gave away the location of where they would be eating late one night and would identify Veldi to the approaching officials with a kiss (no tongues). The trap was set.

Veldi didn't seem surprised when the treachery came:

"Are you betraying the son of Colin with a kiss?"

A gang of heavily armed Inmates burst onto the scene once Veldi had been identified; the target had been marked and the intent was capture.

Veldi did not run. Instead, Veldi went forth to meet them!

The feeling is that the line in the Prison manual above is meant to surprise. But why would Veldi run if he could control everything around him? If Veldi really wanted to evade capture, rather than an undignified escape, hopping over walls in a robe and exposing himself in the process, he could have just given guards the fig tree treatment. Go figger.

At one point Veldi's most trusted sidekick decided that he did not want to *turn the other cheek* or *love his enemies* and cut off the right ear of an Inmate who was part of the arresting party, so a rumble of some description did happen. Veldi healed the Inmate's damaged ear on the spot to show there were no hard feelings. Veldi didn't discriminate against those who were sick and those who wanted him killed. What was he planning?

Veldi was quickly hauled in front of a blood-thirsty kangaroo court and was asked specifically if he was the son of Colin. Veldi blanked the question.

Through a series interrogations and trials he maintained his suicidal silence or gave vague answers which angered the officials to the point of tearing their own clothes, which must have been a lot of anger.

Witnesses were rolled in and out one by one to testify against Veldi. The two main charges were claiming to be Colin's Son and that he was heard to say he would tear down the House of Colin he had previously visited and then rebuild it in three days. This was viewed as blasphemy by the court, who should have realised that Colin built the whole Prison in 6 days, so this was realistically a walk in the park for his Son if the same kind of talent was passed down.

The court eventually decided they'd had enough, and handed down the already agreed sentence – transportation by crucifixion. This would require rubber stamping by a top official to seal Veldi's fate. The problem for the staff was that the official was less than convinced by the outcome of the trials. To try and appease the bloodthirsty staff, he dished out some punishment of his own to Veldi in the hope of putting the whole sorry affair to bed:

The top official took Veldi and had him flogged. Two of the soldiers twisted together a crown of thorns and put it on his head. They clothed him in a purple robe, and went up to him again and again, saying, "Hail, king of the J Wing!" And they slapped him in the face.

Yet, this didn't manage to quell the murderous appetite of the officious requesters.

"We have a law, and according to that law he must die, because he claimed to be the Son of Colin."

The top official seeing that he could not satisfy the staff with his own lesser punishments washed his hands of the situation.

Veldi was to be executed. He first had to haul a heavy wooden cross to his place of destiny still wearing the crown of thorns. Once there, he was attached to the cross by having large nails hammered through his hands and feet, then propped into the upright position to suffer a painful death. Or so it seemed.

C Wing traditionally views the events of Veldi's death on the cross as Veldi acting in his official capacity under Colin. He was willing to sacrifice himself to atone for all of the Prison's sins and make transportation to Dungeon2 possible. The willing part is explained by his lack of defence at the kangaroo courts held to pass down the sentence.

Once dead, Veldi's gophers collected his body and placed it in a tomb. And yet, three days later, the tomb was discovered to be empty. Veldi was back!

Veldi made various cameo appearances for the next forty days to a number of men. He even had lunch with former employees to prove that he was real flesh and blood. Then, at the end of the tour, he vanished off to Dungeon2. Forever and ever, our man.

This was a strange ending to Veldi's time in Colin's Prison. Coming back to life after three days couldn't have rubber-stamped his credentials in the way that is claimed today, as this had already been witnessed previously and people hardly seemed to care. Did Veldi really die the first time around? Could it just be possible that he realised the game was up? After regaining consciousness he visited a few friends before doing a runner? Why couldn't he save himself? A nagging feeling is left that he only performed miracles when he controlled the stage – when the control was taken away, he seemed ineffective. A more realistic explanation for the resurrection of Veldi would be that his followers robbed Veldi's body from the tomb and dumped it elsewhere, thus being able to create the myth and carry on receiving the adulation from certain sections of the Prison. Without a body how could they be proven wrong?

Chapter 5

Colin's Wings

Six main Wings make up the majority of Colin's Prison, with smaller blocks attached.

Each Wing and block is different. There are a variety of channels and methods existing to worship Colin throughout the areas of the Prison, but they all have similar purposes – to keep the Inmates in check through ancient stories and beliefs, and to make threats against non-conformity towards Prisoners who dare to contemplate an alternative. Order must be kept and the Prison maintained.

The records of each main Wing in Prison history contain blemishes and marks of shame against inmatinity that will not be easily erased. None of the Wings have been proven to be innocent through their time in Prison; the claimed purity in the pursuit of Colin's way is laughable. The right choice for any confused Inmate weighing up the options is difficult. No Wing has ever been proven ultimately right and the favoured Wing in Colin's eyes.

It is fair to say though that some Wings are trying a little harder than others to keep themselves out of trouble nowadays.

H Wing

The Hs believe in the sacredness of all life, and that life should not be destroyed violently; perhaps they should spend a bit more time studying Colin's design. A main claim of the Hs is that they follow a vegetarian diet, although this would seem optional. H Wing is the third largest block in Prison and they worship multiple Colins that all form one super Colin, this goes against the mainstream view of a single Colin. H Wing's history has been peaceful compared to the two larger Colin Wings, so criticism is held back. A famous H Wing staff member was a small bespectacled Inmate in a robe who slept between his two nieces whilst naked, to 'avoid' temptation. As you do.

B Wing

The fourth largest Wing in Prison. Most meats can be plated up as long as staff members are not seen slaughtering the animal – leave the dirty work to the Inmates. Colin passed on some direct instructions to the staff of B Wing to avoid eating ten kinds of meats: Inmates, elephants, horses, dogs, snakes, lions, tigers, boars and hyenas. It makes one's stomach turn to think of what was being eaten in this Wing before Colin stepped in. B Wing is also relatively peaceful compared to the big two Wings. The most famous B Wing product is the current Head of staff, not necessarily resident as he spends most of his time in other Wings giving speeches and staying in cushy cells eating club sandwiches.

C Wing

C Wing, the home of Veldi whose manual has here been mainly used for demonstration purposes, lacks most forms of culinary oppression – it's very flexible regarding alcohol and meat. Staff members of C Wing can also slaughter their own animals if they feel the need, although most are confined to choking their chickens in private. C Wing has had wars with other Wings in the name of Colin and throughout history has also suffered lots of bitter infighting and forcible domination of Inmates by leading fanatical staff members. The staff are less vicious in modern times towards adult Inmates, but secretly long for the bygone days of inquisition. The most well-known staff member of C Wing is a revolting old Teutonic virgin preacher who backs Colin policies that have led to millions of transportations. He was part of great war 60 years ago involving all wings.

J Wing

J Wingers only eat animals that have a split hoof and chew their cud, such as sheep, goats and cows. Reptiles and pigs are off the menu. A ritual slaughter has to performed by a staff member on the animal by humanely slicing it's throat; this is apparently painless for the animal as it stands with its head in a strap with a gaping neck wound, bleeding to death. J Wing Inmates will only drink wine made in J Wing. This is not wine snobbery though as it is usually disgusting. A few decades ago, the J Wing population suffered terribly at the hands of barbarian non-believers, although a large percentage of them were known to be attached to C Wing. In fact, the revolting old Teutonic virgin preacher mentioned previously was a confirmed member of the hoard. Veldi was said to be 'King of the J Wingers', but its most famous resident today is a fashion designer who hides his real name. It's doubtful if the clothes would sell as well if the label used went under the name of Ralph Lipshitz. J Wing also cut the foreskin off their children, Colin told them to do it.

I Wing

The dietary laws of I Wing are very close to those of J Wing, but don't tell them that. They forbid eating blood, pork and animals found already dead. Certain parts of I Wing's aim is total Prison domination, considering all other Wings as inferior beings.

Large-scale wars over differing views regarding Colin took place between I and C Wings hundreds of years ago; they are still stewed over today by members of the Wings, and are used as propaganda when whipping up bilious hatred. Areas of I Wing are brutal, and the staff preach intolerance in the name of Colin. They promote attacks against other Wings, and Inmates regularly get early transportation via slaughter of fellow believers along with themselves, in the name of Colin.

Women are treated like second class Prisoners, and have their genitals mutilated in parts of the Wing – a crime against inmatinity. I Wing members pray to Colin five times a day facing Mecca or some other casino like that.

A Wing

There are no dietary laws for A Wing. They do not believe in Colin and do not have his staff overseeing their actions. They are not official Prisoners, though they come under the same umbrella as the rest. Because of what is forced down their throats, it's difficult to escape the tentacles of Colin's Prison whoever you are. A Wing has many famous residents, but a lot of them are assumed to live in C Wing. Closer inspection would prove otherwise. Inmates who worship the word of Colin believe that A Wing members are going straight to Dungeon3.

Chapter 6

Colin's Knaves

Prison had been established, the different laws and beliefs were in place and examples had been set. How could Prison be maintained whilst being taken advantage of?

The design had millions of Inmates in a frightened serf-like state, and was ripe for plucking, manipulating, twisting and all kinds of fraudulent and evil activities. Colin had crafted a place that was perfect for his knaves to flourish. And they did just that, in the name of Colin.

The Prison was a creation of subservience, dictatorship and chicanery.

It's time to look at some of the more interesting characters throughout the history of the Prison who have operated under the illusion of Colin's bidding.

The first two knaves worthy of mention are a pair of Colin's merchants of propaganda from C Wing – Rascal and Apuinas.

Both are described as philosophers, but this is not the right word to use for either of the Prison peddlers. Rascal and Apuinas seemed only ever consider one side of the argument as right, and that side was always Colin's. Anything else would be considered either dangerous or thoughtless. Some three hundred and fifty years ago, Rascal had a wager for non-believers that went along the lines of:

An Inmate must place a bet on Colin existing or not; they couldn't avoid making a selection even if their mind was not made up about Colin. The choices were:

1.   Bet on Colin existing. If a Prisoner wins, they win in big way – an eternal life in Dungeon2 licking Colin's boots. If Colin doesn't exist, then loss is insignificant compared to betting on the other option and getting it wrong.

2.   Bet on Colin not existing. If an Inmate loses this bet, he loses in a big way – an eternal life in Dungeon3, drowning in a cauldron of molten sludge. If Colin doesn't exist, then the Inmate wins the bet but the gain is minimal. They wouldn't even know of their victory.

The first thing to reiterate is that as Rascal was an avid follower of Colin could Inmates really trust his objectivity? The bet could be viewed as designed to make Inmates spend their first sentence in Colin's Prison worshipping the creator whether they believed in him or not. The odds are heavily weighted in Colin's favour.

Not believing in Colin can only bring a slight gain but a massive loss; believing in him could bring huge benefits. A derisory glance at the wager would lead to only one sensible conclusion; yet on further inspection all is not what it seems.

Betting and believing are two different things. The wager assumes that Colin can be forced to be believed by an Inmate for the sake of personal gain. Colin would be able to see into the deceptive mind of the non-believer who pretended to accept his existence.

A lifetime could be spent by a Prisoner pretending to worship Colin, but what would happen when it came to the judgment which defined the next destination? Who would Colin favour when he came to make his decision if he had two non-believers in front of him who took alternative bets? A person living an honest life who had not seen sufficient evidence to form a belief or a liar acting in pure self-interest? Who is the most moral?

Secondly, the bet assumes that the gain would be minimal if a Prisoner went against Colin existing and won. This assumption has not been thought through. If a non-believer took the bet against Colin, it would also mean a lifetime in Prison living outside the clutches of Colin's staff. There would be no need to inhabit a fundamentalist Wing with their laws or to live under the constant shadow of being watched, having their most intimate thoughts read or persistently sinning for unknown reasons. For a non-believer this is a significant gain.

The last problem of the bet is that no Wing is recommended. It's all fine and well to believe in Colin but a channel has to be chosen to carry out the belief. The Wings all have opposing views, so to make a decision on the simple premise of the bet is almost impossible. Rascal must be assuming that the choice would be C Wing as this is where his wager is aimed from. It would have been interesting to see his reaction if an Inmate took the bet on Colin and declared himself as I Wing.

How could anyone know which Wing was telling the truth, as all are different and claim the others are wrong? We know what Rascal thought of the wager from this following quote:

"There are only two kinds of Prisoners we can call reasonable: either those who serve Colin with their whole heart because they know him, or those who search after him with all their heart because they do not know him."

The conclusion must be that Rascal was acting in the name of Colin without his confirmed approval for Rascal's indecent proposal. The philosophical potion being peddled by Rascal was designed to make Inmates who couldn't believe, pretend to believe in Colin. He once said:

"All of inmatity's problems stem from a Prisoner's inability to sit quietly in a room alone."

If only he did.

The second 'philosopher' was named Apuinas and is considered one of C Wing's most famous sages. He was around just over 700 years ago and mused over sexism, domestic violence, masturbation and execution. Below is what this historic cuddly toy of Colin's had to say about non-belief:

"On their own side there is the sin, whereby they deserve not only to be separated from the C Wing by excommunication, but also to be severed from the Prison by death."

Perhaps this was just an honest yet misguided attempt at optimising the Wing? Why would the non-believer even care about being excommunicated from C Wing if they didn't believe the whole story in the first place? Being killed would obviously be more of a serious issue to confront. Apuinas went onto say:

"The Inmate and the master who preside over the Prison household, which is an imperfect community, have imperfect coercive power, which is exercised by inflicting lesser punishments, for instance by blows.

For the sake of completeness it was nice of Apuinas to include an example at the end of this quote on how to manage 'lesser punishments'.

He couldn't exactly be described as a liberal, this is what the cheeky scamp had to say about female Inmates:

"Good order would have been wanting in the human family if some were not governed by others wiser than themselves. So by such a kind of subjection woman is naturally subject to man."

Apuinas could be described as a traditionalist, he continued:

"Woman is defective and accidental and misbegotten, a male gone awry, the result of some weakness in Colin's generative power."

The suspicion is that he has a chip on his shoulder against the female of the species. How did Apuinas think he got into Prison in the first place?

Apuinas didn't shy away from uncomfortable topics and spoke about masturbation with relish:

"By procuring pollution, without any copulation, for the sake of venereal pleasure: this pertains to the sin of 'uncleanness'."

An Inmate who has a personal play is risking the wrath of Colin. As Colin is omniscient, then any Inmate even thinking of trying the next time they are in bed alone and got the urge should stop immediately. Colin will be watching them, and it will be added to their record. In Colin's Prison even the simple pleasures have their risks.

It would be interesting to read Apuinas' Prison record if it ever became available.

Finally on Apuinas, he created a series of lists showing five ways which proved the existence of Colin. Let's look at one of them:

The Fifth Way: Argument from Design

> *1.   We see that natural bodies work toward some goal, and do not do so by chance.*

Some goal? A personal goal? A life goal? Is Apuinas suggesting that Colin controls every Inmate's brain?

> *2.   Most natural things lack knowledge.*

Apuinas himself can't be included in this – Colin's medieval megaphone had an opinion on everything.

> *3.   But as an arrow reaches its target because it is directed by an archer, what lacks intelligence achieves goals by being directed by something of intelligence.*

Are things that lack intelligence always led by something of intelligence? Looking at some of the dog owners in Prison suggests this is not the case.

> *4.   Therefore some intelligent being exists by whom all natural things are directed to their end; and this being we call Colin.*

Now it's clear… Colin is the archer, Prisoners are the arrows and the Dungeons are the moving targets.

***

There are numerous examples of con artists who have acted under the banner of Colin for their own personal financial gain. The most successful of these confidence tricksters have owned large profitable rackets operating on a grand scale.

These powerfully greedy... er, 'gentlemen' make it their personal mission to take advantage of Inmates' fragilities and insecurities to line their own fat pockets. They operate through the media of television and radio to unsuspecting eyes and ears in order to 'spread the word' of Colin through their own institutions.

'Send in your money if you want a free ticket to Dungeon2' they will say. 'Subscribe to our channel if you want to shed your sins' is the claim. 'Give us your pension you gullible old cash-cow' is a decoded version of their dishonest twaddle.

Usually targeted are Inmates of an older age who are close to Colin's apparent judgment or the mentally weak Inmates who are looking for some acceptance and comfort. The richer and more gullible the better as far as the frauds are concerned. Let us look at three of the worst offenders.

Mr Bobbymoon is a prominent example of a C Wing shakedown artist. This unofficial staff member has made a fortune from a very successful extortion racket. He is very forthright with his opinions, take for example this quote:

"I have a zero tolerance for sanctimonious morons who try to scare people."

Well, quite. Mr Bobbymoon must really struggle with self toleration after giving the following prediction that he claimed Colin told him:

"I guarantee you, by the end of 1982 there is going to be a judgment on the Prison."

Of course he didn't mean it really mean it. This can be innocently explained away in Bobbymoon's noble pursuit of cash. Why not scare people and then provide somewhere to turn? To be fair to Bobbymoon, he is very much a traditionalist as his grip on medical science is that of an Inmate living in manualical times:

"I know one man who was impotent, who gave AIDS to his wife and the only thing they did was kiss."

Recently on one of his programmes, he came out with a very interesting quote. A Prisoner phoned in asking for advice concerning a friend. The friend's wife had advanced Alzheimer's disease.

Although the Inmate was caring for her, he had started to see another woman. Here is Bobbymoon's curious response:

"I know it sounds cruel, but if he's going to do something, he should divorce her and start all over again, but make sure she has custodial care and somebody looking after her. If you respect that vow, you say 'til death do us part. This is a kind of death."

It would be nice if Bobbymoon expanded on this confusing piece of advice and provided some enlightenment around the different kind of deaths available.

Another prolific earner was Mr Fellatio, whose piggishness for cash was as almost as remarkable as it was shameless. He successfully gobbled up large amounts of money from the Prisoners, although his business acumen was not as impressive as his scrounging. He once had to sell off a couple of impressive holiday cells and a top of the range car.

Fellatio's excuse for the start of his pillaging was almost as funny as his airbrushed publicity photographs. He claimed he picked up the manual and it mysteriously flicked open to the following passage:

I wish above all things that thou mayest prosper and be in health, even as thy soul prospereth.

Fellatio knew what he was being told from the control room, that it was his mission to be rich. He immediately bought himself an expensive car. Colin appeared to him afterwards and told him he was doing the right thing.

Fellatio built up an impressive empire and set about blowing cash on the finer things in life. But there was a problem – the money was being splurged more quickly than it was being sponged.

Fellatio had a plan up his sleeve to boost his collection. He emotionally pleaded to his television audience for a large fixed amount of money in donations, otherwise Colin was going to, *"...call me home"*. The brazen insinuation was that he was going to die if Inmates did not cough up quickly. Some duped Inmates saw Fellatio's outrageous plot as a suicide threat, as his acting was so convincing. He managed to 'raise' even more than the vast amount he'd set his hungry sights on.

"I heard the voice of Colin. I've heard that voice many times; it's familiar to me, and there's no way that I can fail to understand it's Colin's voice because I'm familiar with it."

Of course he was, although Fellatio's beautiful circular logic is to be admired.

For the sake of impartiality, he did once modestly admit, *"Colin heals, I don't."* Slightly less believable are his claims of seeing a vision of a nine hundred foot tall Veldi who told him to build a hospital, then a normal sized Veldi who instructed Fellatio that he had been officially assigned to find a cure for cancer.

Fellatio lived a luxury lifestyle, always adorned in flash suits and dripping with jewels, even in his times of financial strife. He was eventually 'called home' a decade ago.

The last of this triumvirate of luxuriance is Mr Forwarder whose TV channel requested from its subscribers large sums of money on a weekly basis. The proceeds were used for Forwarder to live an opulent lifestyle and to build and develop a successful theme park.

"Why should I apologise because Colin throws in crystal chandeliers, mahogany floors, and the best construction in the world?"

It's easy to see Forwarder's point about apologising to detractors. If he believed what he preached, then he had to save all of his apologising up for Colin, under the threat of an eternal red hot tribulation at the Prison gates. He attempted to justify himself with the following quote:

"I believe that if Veldi were alive today, he would be on TV."

I believe if Forwarder were alive back then he would have been lynched as a blasphemous thief. The money wasn't all spent on the theme park and a house, though. Forwarder was careful to set a little aside to award himself large bonuses on top of his generous salary, and also took the opportunity to pay off a female Inmate from his organisation after she didn't take too kindly to his attempts to exorcise some pleasure out of her. Forwarder knew what Colin wanted him to do though:

"It's not listed in the Prison manual, but my spiritual gift, my specific calling from Colin, is to be a television talk-show host."

Naturally.

Some of Forwarder's other activities eventually caught up with him, and he was thrown in jail for fraud. On his release, Forwarder's opinion had altered somewhat:

"My heart was crushed to think that I led so many people astray. I was appalled that I could have been so wrong, and I was deeply grateful that Colin had not struck me dead as a false prophet!"

"For making a false profit" would look nice tagged onto the end of his statement. The change was refreshing anyway, but does evidence exist in Prison that Colin strikes people dead for lying? Amusingly he added:

"You know, I try not to look back, because looking forward is so much better than looking backward."

It must be very uncomfortable to do so. Amazingly, Forwarder is currently trying to set up the same kind of scam that originally got him into trouble – which proves he doesn't look backwards at all.

***

Carrying out pure evil in Colin's name against fellow Inmates has always been acceptable in the eyes of some believers. The level of depravity has often varied but there can be absolutely no doubts about it. Three demagogues have made a big impact in Colin's Prison, all in the name of Colin.

They did this by forming breakaway cults in their various Wings by exploiting the deepest deficiencies of Inmates and inflaming popular prejudices. In order to carry out their twisted ideas, brainwashing Inmates to carry out stomach churning acts was the order of the day. Hero worship was obviously par for the course.

Arguably the most vile of these creatures was Awad Bin, who inhabited a murky corner of I Wing until very recently.

Awad Bin planned many mass casualty attacks against J and C Wing. He didn't care if any Wings Inmates were brutally butchered in the process, which makes his following statement appear strange:

"I support any I Wing residents."

If I Wing residents happened to be victims of his attacks he wasn't bothered. They were seen as collateral damage in his quest for improper justice. The following Awad Bin statement is also pitifully contradictive:

"Those who kill our women and innocent, we kill their women and innocent, until they refrain."

By 'our' he means I Wing residents. His own suicide would be understandable if he took his own statements seriously, but like all good demagogues he was above his own fruitcake mandate and never carried out the attacks personally once he won the throne.

Trying to ascertain what he means by 'women and innocent' is also troublesome. Did Awad Bin mean that all women are not innocent? Or was he saying that only a percentage of male Inmates were innocent and female Inmates were not judged? He certainly wasn't against using female Inmates for suicide attacks. Whatever he meant, Awad Bin did not discriminate between Wings or sexes when plotting his cowardly next moves.

Eventually, all of this had to come to an end; soldiers caught up with Awad Bin in a Prison compound where he had been holed. This was his base for carrying out his operations remotely, but this time there was no escape.

Being such a heroic figure, what happened next fits nicely with his profile in general. The brave Awad Bin in a last triumphant act of defiance tried to cower behind a female Inmate to avoid his fate. This didn't work and he was thankfully shot in the face, which ended his term in Colin's Prison. He was previously quoted as saying:

"I'm fighting so I can die a martyr and go to Dungeon2 to meet Colin."

It's nice to think that if this was even possible, Colin angrily threw Awad Bin into Dungeon3. Instead of the seventy-two virgins he was expecting as his reward for his destructive life, he was probably rewarded with seventy-two well-endowed male Inmates who are continually raping him in a pit of boiling slime.

The next maniacal demagogue was Mr Bones, a different breed from Awad Bin but an evil one nonetheless.

He rose through the ranks, starting out as shifty hustler in the name of Colin, all the way to being a drug-crazed tycoon of minor despotism. He was responsible for the largest ever mass suicide in Colin's Prison.

Initially, Bones put on badly staged shows 'healing' people to build his popularity; some Inmates took the rancid bait. Once he'd fooled enough people, he formed his breakaway C Wing cult called 'The Inmates Temple'. This was Bones' vehicle for achieving the endgame. He said:

"To me death is not a fearful thing. It's living that's cursed."

Living was certainly cursed for the people unfortunate enough to fall for Bones' dangerous rambling.

The drug abusing demagogue was obsessed with power. He demanded that all Inmates call him "Father" or "Daddy". But things quickly escalated in his warped mind: Bones started to believe he was a reincarnation of Veldi, and in his last manic years in Prison he actually thought he was Colin.

When rumours started to spread about the terrible conditions in Bones' paradise temple, an official decided to visit to check out the situation. By now the drug taking had taken its toll on Bones and he was in poor health, he viewed the visit as a sign of his own demise. The visiting group was attacked and the official was killed on the order of Bones. The following words were unfortunately a sign of things to come:

"A lot of people are tired around here, but I'm not sure they're ready to lie down, stretch out and fall asleep."

Unfortunately, Bones decided that the Temple was ready to 'lie down' and ordered his beleaguered followers to commit 'revolutionary suicide'. This lead to the death of nine hundred and fourteen Inmates – three hundred and three of them children. They drank a grape-flavoured juice laced with cyanide that Bones and a few of his most loyal followers prepared. Some of his final words were:

"We didn't commit suicide; we committed an act of revolutionary suicide protesting the conditions of an inhumane Prison."

He didn't actually drink the deadly fruit cocktail himself – he was found with a shotgun wound to the head. It is unknown whether it was self-inflicted; we can only hope it wasn't and he lived his final few moments begging in fear.

The eccentric Mr Pearblack is the last of the triple serving from the demagogalogue. In a short space of time, he transformed from being a mild-mannered music teacher into a dangerous oddball and master manipulator.

He formed the bizarre cult 'Dungeon2's Gate', and believed he was related to Veldi, which made him from the:

"Evolutionary Kingdom Level above Inmates"

Pearblack claimed that the Prison was about to be 'recycled', and he had the answer to surviving this purge – immediate self-slaughter.

Dungeon2's Gate was naturally against suicide. What they would perform was a way to get to 'the next Level' and avoid being recycled. Following on from the 'Final Exit', a spaceship closely following a passing comet would pick up the cult members who would become part of the crew. He said of those who would accuse them of taking their own lives:

"Those individuals are ignorant of the evolutionary level above human."

It's difficult to believe how anyone could follow his ideas, though some disastrously did. To help the process along, Pearblack and several other male Inmates got castrated; all got the same haircuts and dressed in the same clothes. The cult hired an area of Prison for the final act, and Pearblack made a short video in which he claimed:

"We do in all honesty hate this Prison."

The thirty-nine dead, including Pearblack, were all found wearing identical clothing and trainers with plastic bags over their heads. They were all individually wrapped in a purple sheet. A mixture of vodka, pineapple and poison had been taken.

This was a rather undignified exit from Colin's Prison, and if they were 'beamed up' it's easy to imagine the strange corpses being quickly returned by the aliens instead of giving them a job on the bridge.

This hideous event goes to show that some Inmates will believe anything, no matter how odd. In the highly unlikely scenario that Pearblack and his followers are whizzing around space in a futuristic craft whilst looking down on Prison with hatred, a humble apology is given.

***

The next category of Colin's knaves is the double dealer. The choice is vast from the Prison staff who haven't exactly practiced what they preached.

Three are used again for illustration purposes.

The first creature, a real life wolf in sheep's clothing is Mr Short.

Short is a self-appointed senior member of Colin's staff who operates out of a large House of Colin. There are numerous stories available regarding his conduct towards his wife, which caused his marriage to end up in divorce. It's said that the female Inmate had to run from Short's house to avoid a merciless beating. The following quote is from this charming man:

"I don't really care how I am remembered as long as I bring happiness and joy to people."

Short was fired from his only honest job for financial irregularities, the next step was to become a senior member of Colin's Prison staff.

Short was well-known for his anti-gay activities, frequently talking about homosexuals in negative ways. He headed marches against same sex marriage, and even claimed he could 'cure' the 'disease'. He was once described as the most homophobic staff member in Prison. He claimed:

"We touch a lot of Prisoners. This is a Prison-impacting ministry, and I personally get a little offended when my integrity is questioned."

He did touch a lot of Prisoners as it turned out. Four Inmates filed lawsuits against Short for abusing his staff position in order to lure them into abusive sexual relationships.

Short paid his accusers wages with money gained from his House of Colin to soften them up. He bought them expensive gifts and took them on holidays overseas. One described a creepy candlelit ceremony that the 'anti-gay' Short performed: He quoted the word of Colin and exchanged jewels in a fake wedding. Short denied everything:

"I have devoted my life to helping others and these false allegations hurt me deeply. But my faith is strong and the truth will emerge. All I ask for is your patience as we continue to categorically deny each and every one of these ugly charges."

As the pressure ramped up on Short and the evidence was becoming damning, he decided to change his tone:

"I am not a perfect man, but this thing, I'm going to fight."

Is this the closest you can get to an admission of guilt from a desperate megalomaniac? Short, like most of the other shysters who have made a bundle on the back of Colin, had no other option but to settle out of court, as the details being made public would have destroyed him forever. It would almost be funny if victims weren't involved. Short will need deep pockets as more lawsuits are heading in his direction.

Mr Smashers is one of the knaves that can be laughed at without too much guilt. Apart from condoning the beating of children and the odd strange idea, Smashers was Mister Squeaky Clean.

He was another one of Colin's staff who had strong views in line with his beliefs regarding homosexuality. He classed it as a 'gender disturbance'; he knew a cure through:

"The positive therapeutic effects of religious conversion for curing transsexualism."

Even though his opinions were a touch peculiar, he took part in a number of trials as an 'expert' in homosexuality matters. From defending the boy scout movement to gay adoption, if a witness was needed to discuss the terrible impurities of this kind of behaviour is was Smashers.

It turned out that Smashers was more of an 'expert' than most thought. He was photographed leaving an airport with a rent-boy after arriving back from a holiday overseas. His claim that he hired the young man to carry his luggage because of an injury is priceless in value, especially as the photo showed him clearly carrying his own suitcase out of the airport. Smashers spluttered:

"If you talk with my travel assistant, you will find I spent a great deal of time sharing scientific information on the desirability

of abandoning homosexual intercourse, and I shared the Gospel of Veldi with him in great detail."

In a subsequent interview, the rent-boy didn't hold back and told all. Smashers hired him from a well-known website set up for prostitution-type activities. Whilst overseas, the rent-boy was instructed to give Smashers naked massages which included his private parts.

Smashers claimed that he 'interviewed' a few people for the role as 'travel assistant' and had no idea of the rent-boy's history.

Who was to be believed? Smashers fired out an impetuous email in his defence:

"I confessed to the Lord and to my family that I was unwise and wrong to hire this travel assistant after knowing him only one month before the trip and not knowing whether he was more than a person raised in a C Wing home."

Guilty as sin.

Mr Constralis completes the set of three, his story is astonishing. Not only was he another one of Colin's staff, he also wrote C Wing rock songs. All innocent enough at first glance.

Life seemed good for Constralis as he toured around a small part of Prison belting out Colin-inspired music, until one day a terrible tragedy struck.

After picking up a minor injury he was admitted to hospital for treatment. On his exit from hospital, Constralis tearfully announced that he was suffering from terminal cancer. A terrible body blow for any Inmate to receive.

The disease appeared to take a hold of Constralis quickly; he was visibly in agony and his hair loss was uncomfortable to watch for those around him. His father, also one of Colin's staff, had a special air conditioned room made for the stricken crooner, and openly wept at services he conducted whilst begging for his son to be cured.

Constralis decided he was not going to take this lying down though. He produced a musical song called 'Healer' about his battle with the terrible disease. The song was a smash hit, and for the next eighteen months Constralis bravely ploughed on performing 'Healer' to larger crowds. This was picked up around the whole Prison and his popularity soared to new heights. He was held up as glowing example of dignity. He also toured Houses of Colin and gave tear-drenched readings from the Prison manual to captivated followers.

Constralis was still evidently suffering with hair loss, and quite often he had to perform his uplifting song with an oxygen tube up his nose. Some of the lyrics from his song were:

You hold my every moment

You calm my raging seas

You walk with me through fire

And heal all my disease.

Constralis' father eventually decided he could take no more. His father wasn't upset seeing his son struggle through the concerts with the assistance of oxygen or watching him slip away from Colin's Prison through a terrible disease, his objection was of a different nature.

Constralis' father publicly admitted that his son was lying and did not have, and never did have, cancer.

It emerged that Constralis shaved his own hair off, borrowed medical equipment and had been sending bogus emails to himself from imaginary medical staff to fool everyone and keep the lie going. Constralis said:

"I don't know how you can fake vomiting all over yourself night after night after night, I'm not that good an actor."

Perhaps it was from drinking large amounts of alcohol from the record profits? The real story was that Constralis was heavily addicted to pornography, and had been 'battling' this for sixteen years. He eventually admitted that he never did have cancer, but made the claim that it was the porn that made his body break down because he was sinning.

The final knave in this identification line of wonderment is a senior staff member from Colin's Prison who deserves a category of his own.

This is the most influential staff member in C Wing; the position has been held for centuries by various different kinds of characters and is simply known as the 'Dope'.

The current holder of the title, Dope Ratslinger is a spooky Teutonic virgin. He was also a member of a barbarian hoard who decimated the ranks of J Wing. His stories about being part of one of the most evil armies to have existed in Prison are worth taking a look at. What else could he say apart from that he never really agreed with the policies but was just 'following orders'? His tales of desertion and handing himself over to the opposition look like they back up his claims. But do they?

Ratslinger only 'deserted' after his unit was disbanded. So what did he actually 'desert' from? This was done at the point where the war mentioned in the C Wing description was lost, units were broken up, the soldiers told to go home, and it was every Prisoner for himself.

So how did Ratslinger hand himself over to the opposition? This claim is made to try and show that he didn't agree with the evil army and decided to surrender himself to the other side – the side that was on the brink of victory and would shortly expose disgusting crimes against inmatinity to the whole Prison. What actually happened was that he went home. Just as he arrived, the opposition army swept through his town and made his family's house their local headquarters. Ratslinger was caught, arrested and thrown into a Prisoner of war camp.

It's understandable that Ratslinger had to create a purposely vague cover-up if he wanted to fly through the ranks to the top position.

There was a chilling irony to the confirmation of Ratslinger as the new Dope. Names were burned in a furnace and white smoke belched out of chimney to signal that he had been elected. Sixty years previously, those names were real Inmates being massacred by the army which Ratslinger was a part of – the smoke back then signalled genocide.

Ratslinger seems untroubled about having death on his hands. He carries on refusing to go against one of his sect rules in C Wing that condoms should not be used in order to help stopping the spread of fatal diseases. This had led to hundreds of thousands of deaths across the Prison – Inmates who have followed the words of him and former Dopes and have died from disease as a consequence. Is there any guilt displayed by the Dope? It appears not. He said of the problem:

"The problem cannot be overcome by the distribution of prophylactics: on the contrary, they increase it."

The first part is right – prophylactics will not overcome the disease alone; the second part is highly questionable. His justification was that handing out condoms would encourage sex in Prison. One of his solutions was that people shouldn't have sex.

That's ok for him to say; we all know he can apparently live without it (although it would only be truly believable if he passed a polygraph test). His predecessor Dope Apaul also took the same line and said:

"Stupidity is also a gift of Colin, but one mustn't misuse it."

How is stupidity used correctly?

Apaul was also reluctant to expose the child sex abuse rife amongst the staff members of his cult. Eventually, under intense pressure, he slowly reacted. It is estimated that around five thousand of his staff members have carried out this crime under his watch.

It would be easy to dwell on the last two Dopes and pick away at all of their faults, but some more interesting and strange staff have held this position in Prison history.

Take Dope Steve for example, the unofficial holy king of spite. If awards were being handed out for holding a grudge against a former boss, Steve would be in line for the top prize.

He despised his predecessor so much that he had his decomposing body dug up after nine months, dressed in the Dapal robes and the corpse was then put on trial. The corpse struggled to put up a convincing counter argument to the fictitious charges and was found guilty. The punishment was grotesque, if the scene wasn't enough already. The unfortunate corpse had three of its fingers cut off, was then stripped of its robes and dragged through the streets before being unceremoniously dumped into a nearby river.

Dope Clergius didn't let any staff member or rule stand in his way. He was desperate to be the Dope, only there was a slight problem: applications for the role were currently closed. To make the position vacant again so he could fill it, he arranged for the standing Dope to be strangled to death. Once installed as the new Dope, Clergius went on to have an affair with the daughter of an aristocrat and they had a child together. The son must have inherited his genes – he also managed to manipulate himself into the highest C Wing job.

Dope Ugliface saw his position as the ultimate in Prison. Colin may have been his boss, but he was in no doubt who the Prisoners had to answer to; he wrote:

"Every Prisoner is subject to the Dontiff."

Ugliface viewed himself as the unquestionable top physical presence and overlord of all things penal. He imposed heavy taxes on the Prison population, and argued bitterly with senior Inmates who would not cough up or follow his decrees. He was also put on trial after his death, but this time the corpse wasn't dug up.

The Dope inhabits an impressive part of C Wing, and many of the previous owners of the title are buried there. When visiting other parts of the Prison, the Dope often tours around in a small cart with thick glass as protection for Prisoners.

Colin's knaves come in all kinds of shapes, sizes, capacities and ways. The glittering members featured are only a sample of what has been introduced thanks to Colin. Praise Colin.

Chapter 7

Colin's Seven Deadly Sins

Colin's rules are complimented in the Prison manual by a list of deadly, or cardinal, sins. The sins give an extra indication about what Colin despises – in other words, what could potentially get an Inmate into serious trouble (or what trouble he could imagine himself in). Modern non-manual reading Inmates probably wouldn't recognise the original seven. They have been reworked since the Prison manual was written, but we'll come to a modified set shortly. What is most interesting when browsing the list is how much the sins all actually relate very closely to Colin's knaves and their associates.

Six things that Colin hateth, and the seventh Colin detesteth:

  1. *A proud look.*

It's very rare to see one of Colin's staff looking scruffy; the opposite is usually the true. The higher the rank, the higher the bling is generally the case. Just look at the Dope's hat, the richly woven cloaks, the jewelled staffs and the exotic robes that staff saunter around in. The clothes are designed to stand out and draw attention.

At nearly every official function, when looking at the attendees it's never hard to spot one of Colin's senior staff members muscling in and trying to be the centre of attention. Most Prisoners are wearing soberly coloured jackets or coats; Colin's staff, though, are adorned in expensively made and dazzling purple, cream and yellow robes that are embroidered with a variety of precious gems. Their hats are equally as outrageous and finish off the look – a proud one in their eyes.

2. *A lying tongue.*

Examples have already been put forward for this, but the options are endless when looking at Colin's staff. Lying deviants, adulterers and murderers, selectivity cannot be used as an accusation when choosing from the enormous mass of candidates available. Step forward Mr Notgent, the slippery servant of Colin who ended up in court after a female Inmate was murdered. Her body was found under the floor in his chapel. He eventually admitted to having an affair with the Inmate but his excuse was pathetic:

"She felt more strongly about me than I did about her and it was she who instigated everything. It was not me."

This sounds like something a child in the Prison playground would say when caught punching a girl, not a supposedly pious staff member who was fully aware of his responsibilities. Notgent didn't carry out the murder but he knew where the body was and took full advantage of the free pass this gave him. When asked why he didn't notice his lover was missing and buried in his own House of Colin, he burbled:

"My only explanation is that I may have been drinking."

Then he admitted to being an alcoholic. In a final concession, Notgent claimed he had another affair with a female Inmate who played the guitar in his House of Colin, she denied it ever happened.

3.   *Hands that shed innocent blood.*

It would be easy to simply name the Dope or Awad Bin as examples of mass murder, but it would be wrong to not include Khillmeini somewhere in proceedings. It is true that he is not a part of C Wing where this sin is described, but the general rule still applies in the I Wing manual (if you choose to interpret it nicely); everyone is still part of Colin's Prison and there is no conclusive proof who is right or wrong. When he became the senior staff member in his area of I Wing, he implemented a strict and barbaric law for Inmates to follow. Any Inmate or local staff member who opposed this would usually be brutally butchered or hung by the neck from a large mechanical crane until dead. This lovely bundle of joy said:

"Those who are trying to bring corruption and destruction to our Wing in the name of democracy will be oppressed. They are worse than J Wingers, and they must be hanged. We will oppress them by Colin's order and Colin's call to prayer."

Khillmeini got a little bit upset when somebody suggested democracy should be used to appoint senior Inmates:

"I shall kick their teeth in. I am appointing the senior Inmates. I am appointing the senior Inmates by the support of this Prison!"

A lot of the victims who died on his orders would have preferred to have had their teeth kicked in; they didn't have that option unfortunately.

Khillmeini hated opposition of any kind and went about systematically destroying any dissenting voices. It didn't just stop with the individual though – he made sure their families suffered as well. Any ethnic minority that didn't see his point of view was also put to the sword.

He died just over a couple of decades ago after years or terror, but it's worth remembering this quote when trying to work out his method of rationalisation:

"An Inmate has sex with an edible animal like a sheep, cow, or camel it should be killed and burned. If it is one of the animals which is not usually eaten but is used for riding and transportation, like a horse or donkey, it should be taken out of the block and sold in another block."

Glad he cleared that one up for us.

4. A heart that devises wicked plots.

Amen's heart devised many wicket plots, though not that many at first. When he originally seized power as a senior member of staff it was for all the usual despotic but not necessarily murderous reasons; but the descent was rapid. He quickly installed military law and found it a very useful tool for disposing of any dissenting voices – an I Wing speciality. These included not only political, intellectual or foreign Inmates but also ethnic groups who he didn't particularly like.

"In any block there must be Prisoners who have to die. They are the sacrifices any block has to make to achieve law and order."

It will come as no surprise that not only was he the cause of thousands of innocent Inmate deaths, his self-delusion was astronomically large:

"I consider myself the most powerful figure in the world."

Amen awarded himself undeserved bravery medals, academic qualifications and gave himself ludicrous titles which were unrepeatable in a single breath. This wasn't all as simple as it seems though, Amen purposely created the image of a fool to keep the full scale of his atrocities from being revealed. As wicket plotting goes, Amen was up there. Eventually he was exposed, but justice was never served – he fled his block and lived a quiet life in exile.

5. Feet that are swift to run into mischief.

'Mischief', a petty word when thinking about the corruption, greed, evil and hatred that has been created by Colin.

The Nestboro House of Colin takes mischief to new and degrading levels. The strange and repulsive members enjoy protesting in some of the most distasteful ways imaginable. They are led by a grubby charlatan named Phelps.

They have picketed at the funerals of two Inmate soldiers holding up signs saying 'Colin hates fags' and 'Thank Colin for dead soldiers'. Phelps said:

"Our attitude toward what's happening with the war is that Colin is punishing this evil Prison for abandoning all moral imperatives that are worth a dime."

They also protested at the funerals of a homosexual who was kicked to death on the street and a heavy metal singer. These events for the Nestboro toads are regular occurrences, and the vitriol is weapons grade. Phelps says of these:

"Funerals are the right place. Colin has killed them. The Inmate shouldn't be there dead. But this is the Colin that

delivered ten different plagues – and nothing worked. So here we are."

The Nestboro closet homosexuals also have interesting views on most of the Wings in Prison. They see the Dope as the 'Godfather of paedophilia' and accuse his staff of sucking semen out of junior Inmates' balls like a vampire sucks blood from its targets. All of the Dope followers are going to Dungeon3 apparently.

I-Wing also comes in for some harsh criticism. Their prophet, according to Nestboro, is a demon-possessed whoremonger. One of the ugly offspring of the leader said after she picketed an I Wing funeral:

"All those angry little I Wingers can just shut their mouths."

They did have some advice to offer H Wing, after previously calling them all idle and worthless:

"If you would stop worshipping false Colins, being a fag would not be a complex matter. Stop going a whoring after other Colins and start serving the Living Colin in truth!"

Nestboro save the most amount of bile for J Wing. They have picketed J Wing institutions with signs saying "Colin hates Js" and "Js killed Veldi". On their website it says:

"The only true J Wingers are C Wingers. The rest of the people who claim to be J Wing aren't, and they are nothing more than typical, impenitent sinners ... the vast majority of J Wing supports fags."

The Nestboro House of Colin has a stream of petty opinions on a wide area of topics. They are now banned from even visiting certain parts of Prison because of their 'mischief'. All in the name of Colin.

They may one day get what they deserve, hopefully.

6.   *A deceitful witness that uttereth lies.*

Duckings was the Witchfinder General just over 400 years ago. His father and brother were both official Prison staff but he had other duties, namely the torture and death of around three hundred female Inmates who he claimed were witches. Duckings was very well paid for his 'work', and travelled around a small part of the Prison using an array of strange techniques to keep his scam going.

He would use his female companions to prick people to see if they bled, or would pretend to slash an Inmate's arm with a blunt knife to prove they wouldn't bleed in order to get a conviction. Sleep deprivation was another favoured method to draw out a confession. The worst technique of all was when he would tie an Inmate to a chair and throw her into a river: If the Inmate floated then she was a witch. It's easy to guess what innocence meant. The mark of the devil was also a sign to Duckings to push for a swift execution; this mark would have been a simple mole or birthmark.

Why did he carry out these transparent acts of pure evil? The answer was simple: He was handsomely paid in expenses by each town he visited, one even had to put taxes up to foot the bill.

Just another coin-gluttonous villain carrying out Colin's work.

7. Him that soweth discord among brethren.

It's eight AM on Saturday morning, a few drinks have been consumed the night before. A headache and dry mouth are keeping the Inmate's tired body awake. *Knock, knock, knock!* Who can that be at the cell door this early in the morning on a weekend? It must be important… Bad news? A special delivery? Better run downstairs to find out. Through the frosted glass two people in suits can be seen. Is it the bailiffs? Not behind on any payments, so is it detectives? Done nothing wrong, so maybe not.

The door is opened and the Inmate is met by two falsely pasted-on smiles from men standing on the doorstep holding cheaply printed leaflets. "What do you think Colin would make of Prison today?" they ask. Groan.

These people are Colin's minor staff who think it is their duty to try and brainwash non-believers into their various cults. It has actually worked on a very tiny percentage of people who invite them in for the full show. More often than not the tongue is bitten and a polite 'no thank you' is given before shutting the door. They loiter for a few seconds in the same position in a silent protest at any rebuttal, then move along to disturb the next unsuspecting Inmate. By nine AM, the whole neighbourhood brethren have had the same treatment and are equally as unimpressed by the relatively harmless twerps. The discord has been soweth and a bad mood resides over this part of the block for a short time afterwards.

***

The revised list of the seven deadly sins is cut down to single words.

1. Lust

On top of the podium with a gold medal around their necks are the staff of C Wing, particularly the Dope's cult. The cases of sex abuse number into the many thousands. These sickening lizards who spread the name of Colin and hear Inmates' sins have regularly abused their position to sexually assault children and vulnerable females. The crimes often went unreported for years, the victims embarrassed and scared, the staff sly and quiet. It was all swept under the carpet as long as nobody knew.

It wouldn't help to list any examples of what these chilling weirdos carried out, but the evidence is unquestionable. The excuses and investigations from the senior staff were also miserable; if the staff are as genuine as they claim then the shame must be unbearable. It's sadly doubted.

2. Gluttony

Step forward Mr Blaggart, whose insatiable appetite for prostitutes was almost as intense as his hunger for money and fame through the use of Colin. Blaggart was the typical, immoral, two-faced confidence trickster who appears on television preaching what he did not practice. This wretched specimen even had the nerve to give the following crocodile tear-drenched admission on television after he was caught the first time with a hooker. He should have got an Oscar nomination:

"I have sinned against You, my Colin, and I would ask that your precious blood would wash and cleanse every stain until it is in the seas of Colin's forgiveness, not to be remembered against me anymore."

The next time he was caught it was different – he was still in the game trying to clean up under the flag of Colin, and was in no mood to make a turkey out of himself again. He said to his members:

"The Lord told me it's flat none of your business."

Blaggart is still plying his trade as a master pick-pocket to anyone who will listen. He now says:

"You can't lie to God – it's ridiculous."

He is ridiculous.

3. Greed

Mr Zonk was greedy. Like any good egotistical maniac who builds a gigantic House of Colin, he harvested wages and pensions from his 'flock'. But despite his astoundingly self-righteous preaching, he was also greedy for male penis.

Zonk was eventually exposed by a male prostitute for his behind the scene activities. He had been paying the male prostitute over a period lasting three years for demonic sex sessions. Zonk also bought crystal methamphetamine for personal usage from the Inmate. As he saw his empire at risk, he started to get desperate:

"I did not have a homosexual relationship with a man, I am steady with my wife. I'm faithful to my wife, I have never done drugs."

His fellow shakedown artists initially tried to defend Zonk, but the male prostitute had a voicemail recording of the slimy Zonk asking for the drugs. He still tried to worm his way out of it:

"I bought it for myself but never used it. I was tempted but I never used it."

Eventually, the evidence was so overwhelming that Zonk had to admit all and was sacked. Allegations also surfaced from a young man from his former workplace that seemed irrefutable; Zonk had sexually assaulted him a number of times. The gigantic House of Colin had to pay the young man off. Zonk was clearly repentant:

"Back in the old days when somebody would get in trouble, they'd just need to move 40 or 50 miles, or a hundred miles, and they could start again. Not anymore."

He still desperately goes around trying to drain society of its hard-earned money and claims his attraction to men has amazingly vanished. His excuse for the encounter with the male prostitute was a simple massage that went wrong.

There's more chance of a dinosaur laying an egg on a mermaid's stomach than Zonk telling the truth.

4. Sloth

Colin hates laziness. Not the type of laziness that means sitting in a desert for forty days and nights or in a crypt for three days. Colin hates lazy workers:

Whoever is lazy in his work becomes brother to one who destroys. He breaks again the command of Colin.

Most of Colin's staff are lazy; they let Colin do all of their thinking for them. They parrot the words of the manuals, refuse to contemplate reasonable alternatives to their received opinions and even worthlessly delve into politics to give unoriginal offerings.

The bloated pie eater and swindler Mr Dropbad was one such example. He backed an apartheid regime, claimed a popular children creation named Tinky Winky was designed as a gay role model and, most sickening of all, condoned an atrocious attack against his own block by I Wing terrorists.

"I really believe that the pagans, and the abortionists, and the feminists, and the gays and the lesbians who are actively trying to make that an alternative lifestyle, I point the finger in their face and say 'you helped this happen'."

The fat creep also stated the attacks were "probably deserved." If Dungeon3 exists, he's busy booking his place.

5. Wrath

Mr Immoler was a particularly nasty sheriff of doom around four hundred years ago. Under the beastly instructions of his block ruler Scary, he oversaw the execution of three hundred fellow C Wing Inmates. They were from a C Wing cult whose leader had died and Scary had replaced; she was a follower of the Dope and so was

Immoler. The revenge for this 'heresy' was horrifying; it was written of him:

"This cannibal in three years' space three hundred Inmates slew. They were his food, he loved so blood, he spared none he knew."

Burning at the stake was the standard method for those found guilty in public. People tried to stand up for what Immoler was carrying out at the time by saying 'he was just following orders'. It was a contemptible excuse that has unfortunately echoed through the centuries after, most notably from Inmates who carried out the extermination of millions of J Wing members, as talked previously when discussing Ratslinger.

Immoler's reign did not last as his ruler died and a member of the previous cult took charge again. He was thrown into jail and died shortly afterwards. Perhaps his burning was being saved for Dungeon3?

6. Envy

The envy displayed towards A Wing members is often remarkable. Certain Wings can't accept that a Wing exists that does not believe in Colin. Demands are made that A Wing members must make a choice, or they are mocked and jeered because of what they believe in. Below are a number of quotes which demonstrate the point:

Hurray said: *"A-Wingism is a wonderful philosophy of life as long as you are big, strong, and between the ages of eighteen and thirty-five. But watch out if you are in a lifeboat and there are others who are younger, bigger, or smarter."*

Paidrule babbled: *"Colin exists whether or not Prisoners may choose to believe in Him. The reason why many Prisoners do not believe in Colin is not so much that it is intellectually impossible to believe in Colin, but because belief in Colin forces that thoughtful person to face the fact that he is accountable to such a Colin."*

Endsoft burbled: *"A-Wingism is a crutch for those who cannot bear the reality of Colin."*

Fowler ranted: *"Still, even the most admirable of A-Wingists is nothing more than a moral parasite, living his life based on borrowed ethics. This is why, when pressed, the A-Winger will often attempt to hide his lack of conviction in his own beliefs behind some poorly formulated utilitarianism, or argue that he acts out of altruistic self-interest."*

Stone waffled: *"The worst moment for the A-Winger is when he is really thankful, and has nobody to thank."*

There are many more quotes that run along similar lines. If A Wing people are not acting in an irresponsible way and living as good Inmates, the comments would seem to be born out of jealousy, tinged with irritation that A Wing members have not chosen to be answerable to Colin.

If it's all about eternal salvation then why do these Prisoners even care? They speak as if being factual, when there is no concrete proof either way about Colin.

If A Wingers are comfortable that they do not have to live under the moral code of Colin to know the difference between right and wrong, shouldn't the Prisoners who feel the need be more of a concern? What would they do without it?

Are the above statements a self-defence mechanism against subconscious feelings from the Colin believers? Possibly so. Colin's moral code, though, can be bent to make any argument, to suit any cause.

The envy is against Prisoners who can live perfectly well without believing in Colin.

7. Pride

It's hard not to bitterly laugh when looking at the description of 'pride' when relating it to Colin's staff and senior Inmates. Pride as a sin is seen as being self-absorbed, the wish to be more important or attractive than other Prisoners and failing to acknowledge good things that are not done by oneself.

The dress worn by the staff, the constant gush of pious opinions and the persistent disparagement of others who do not hold the same views about Prison all fit into the description of this sin. The staff's own sense of self-worth is of Olympic proportions.

To stand in front of television cameras and large audiences in order to tell them what they should believe, otherwise they will suffer for eternity, takes a certain amount of arrogance. To think one is always right requires a degree of self-importance, while casting judgment over non-believers is also incredibly contemptuous.

Chapter 8

The Colin Debate

The Prison is real enough from a psychological point of view, but is Colin?

There is a popular debate over Colin's existence today that rages away. It usually boils down to where the burden of proof lies. This book is not attempting to ape those arguments in any way, and Prisoners with far more in-depth knowledge have crossed swords over the issue. But the following is observed:

Believers can point to the Prison manuals as proof but the manuals are only a collection of written texts. It would seem foolish to say, "Well it's in the manual so it must be true" and cast all other opinions aside. The C Wing manual seems like a very early attempt to explain the Prison in a typically superstitious way that would be expected from the times of its drafting. Colin was blamed for most unexplainable things like disease and natural disasters. As the layers have been stripped away through scientific breakthroughs and understanding, the arguments become more obscure, an example of the argument between an A and C Wing residents being:

A: Colin was blamed for plagues in the Prison manual, but it has since been discovered that bacteria was the cause, another reason to know it's all a lie.

C: Well, Colin created everything in the Prison so he must have created the bacteria as well.

A: Now you're being silly; we know that bacteria was one of the first life forms in Prison and you can find it in the Prison's crust.

C: As I said, Colin created the Prison.

A: No he didn't. Prison was formed from a solar nebula; you can't even explain how he took any part in creation of the Prison.

C: OK then, what was there before nothing? Who started it all? What was the force? Do you think it was all just a random accident that we are here now bickering about this?

A: Yes, I do think it was random biology for us in particular. Who was there before Colin to create him?

And so on and so on, until the level where proof is impossible and both sides claim victory. It's possible that Inmates will never know how life actually started. Even if something was found, it would be argued that Colin was there before it or created it. So pointing to the sky for justification from either side is, at the moment fatuous, as the positions are established and the proof is absent.

Natural evolution is not even worth visiting; the attempt to justify the poor and outdated philosophy in the Prison manuals is weak. The manuals are not explaining in metaphor what is understood today. When the manuals were written, their explanations were aligned to the understanding of the time. Inmates believed literally, and the authors had no power to see into the future or the past. The same principle applies to Veldi's miracles, and can also be levelled at any believers who use the more evasive parts of the manuals as excuses for all kinds of warped actions. The manuals have to be taken as a whole; which leads to the next question:

If Colin does exist, why did he create lots of different, bizarre and opposing channels as ways to worship him? This seems a very troubling aspect, one that leads to the conclusion that Colin is a completely Inmate-made invention.

When the Wings eventually burst into life, the leaders were some of the most powerful people in Prison and provided the back-up required for senior Inmates to run their sections of the Prison. What appears to be the case is that Colin has provided an effective form of social control: When laws were being formed and subsequently policed, Colin was a handy tool to have around. He also provided justification for all kinds of behaviour towards Inmates in order to keep them in check. Behaviour through fear. The Wings and associated cults drum into children from an early age the ways of Colin. *Get them early while they are still impressionable* is the philosophy.

What would happen if children were not taught about Colin? Would they miss him? Doubtful. Would they search for him? Even more doubtful. Would they turn into a murdering thieves because of the lack of teaching? No. Prisoners had their own society established before the main Wings stepped in to carry out the conversion.

Colin was also used when attempts were being made to makes sense of the Prison around them by Inmates. He helped to explain the unexplainable by filling in all of the gaps. The unexplained areas have now shrunk, leaving ever smaller holes. Some will always remain unpluggable to keep Colin alive, but the net is slowly closing.

If an Inmate attempted to write a Prison manual today and claimed it as a Wing he would be ridiculed, which has happened. So what makes the popular manuals so true when Inmates wrote them hundreds of years ago with only a tiny understanding of the Prison compared to today? Is it all true because it's old? Which one does Colin back?

If Colin exists, is he comfortable with such disorganisation and conflict within the Prison because of the Inmate beliefs? One supposes that the overall design could back up this point because the Prison's destruction is assured. Why would Colin care if he was around billions of years before Prison and will be for billions of years after? He could try his luck with another Prison perhaps? Maybe that's what Inmates can all see in the distance?

Physical Prison creation will have to remain unknown for the foreseeable future, but this does not authenticate any particular Wing. The burden of proof around the Wings is squarely on the shoulders of the followers. To ask a non-believer to prove a farfetched story that allegedly took place centuries ago didn't happen is to drolly shake off their own responsibilities. The non-believers are not the ones advancing seemingly impossible occurrences as fact.

Is it a coincidence that all of the manifestly absurd events happened when no technology existed to capture what was happening? Why have they not happened since? If Colin really wanted to provide a message of his existence, would it not have been better to have waited a few more thousand years when no arguments could be made against him? Colin apparently waited hundreds of thousands anyway, so it would have only been a blink of an eye in terms of his life.

An infantile counter argument would be that Colin sends signs through prisonquakes or disease. Both have been explained scientifically to a more than acceptable level. This is the point where the follower will take an opponent down the rat-hole of creation again. The argument always ends up being dragged to the same place as it's where the truth is unknown. This is not good enough when justifying a cult and its behaviour in Colin's Prison.

Implausible claims without proof should not be expected to be believed. Having faith in the implausible should not be expected to command immediate respect.

Chapter 9

Life Without Colin

It would be wrong to deny some of the good that the Colin worshipping Wings have brought to the Prison. They have provided a lot of comfort and guidance to millions of Inmates, but their activities are not exclusive through the worship of Colin. A Wing can carry out the very same activities. There is nothing physically a Colin worshipper can do for the good that a non-believer cannot.

Unfortunately, Colin worship has also provided the springboard for corruption, loss of significant life and millions of Inmates living under the Colin stamped hammer of fear and oppression. There are many evil things that are done in the name of Colin that are not carried out by A Wing members. That is the difference. This is not to deny that in Prison history nasty things have been carried out by non-believers, but measuring the two against each other is like comparing a whale to a shrimp.

The pro-Colin arguments are that a moral code has been provided for Inmates to live under, that non-believers are borrowing their morals but don't commit to abide by them as they want convenient lives without any official boundaries. This suggestion is silly for a number of reasons: Firstly, Wing moral code is only adhered to when convenient to its followers; this has already been demonstrated, and the cases number in the millions throughout Prison history.

Secondly, it can't be a serious suggestion that Prisoners would go around raping, pillaging and murdering without the code. If it was true, how did society even survive to reach the point of being submerged into the Wings?

Non-believers are just as capable as believers of doing wicked things as stated. But they would not carry out the wicked activities in the name of an unprovable entity or use him as justification for their actions. This is a key point when considering Colin's Prison for the trouble and death it has caused throughout the centuries.

Thirdly, more and more the Colin-following Wings are becoming outdated as society evolves, while A Wing is the fastest growing. Their members do not go around subjecting Inmates to subtle threats to fall into line or else, they do not bring physical terror to the doorstep of other Wings, carry out brainwashing or hand out dangerous archaic advice that could lead disastrous consequences for the Inmate concerned. If the Wings didn't exist then neither would the mind-forged manacle of Prison. Colin would at most be relegated to a singular metaphor for the unexplained in creation.

Another argument is that Colin would be replaced with evil Colinless dictators, physical ones who would make the Prison a worse place than before. But this is not sensible and has no modern precedent, not in the civilised Prison anyway. The increasing likelihood is that certain blocks will be taken over by angry I Wing groups after their current dictators fall. The evidence today in Prison suggests this offers no improvement.

In some areas, brutal dictators have made themselves Colins, but this was only after taking over an already subservient Prison population that was previously under Colin's thumb – a demagogue's dream, now exposed for all of its ugly falseness. This is unlikely to happen today on a large scale, no matter how hysterically it's put forward by Colin's staff (whose vested interests would be compromised). It could be advanced that Colin is an evil dictator himself, the difference being that he will never die or be deposed, at least not in the minds of his Prisoners.

Just look at how the staff behaved when they did have real power in Prison. Inmates could be burned at the stake for not believing, or cruelly tortured into 'confessing' their sins. Prisoners could also be condemned to death for being a witch, having sex the wrong way or simply not even being liked.

Thankfully those days are behind Inmates as the power of the staff has waned in most areas of Prison apart from certain blocks of I Wing.

An idea would be no Wing having the ability to influence power and no dictator in charge. It would be interesting to see the first realistic attempt without crushing oppression, threats of eternal ownership and unavoidable staff members telling Prisoners how to act in matters of which they have no experience. There would be true freedom to explore every aspect of what is around without being harangued by Colin worshippers; more importantly there would be a license to create a sensible set of laws to suit the society of the day based on logical modern philosophies. Will Inmates ever see it? Not for a few generations at least, but the poison ivy of Colin's Prison is starting to recede.

Colin followers will sneer and say it will lead to hedonism, anarchy and disaster but this is to ignore the innate Prisoner compassion, solidarity and sense of fairness. These things are not taught by a manual or staff members, they already exist within.

Printed in Great Britain
by Amazon.co.uk, Ltd.,
Marston Gate.